GAM

DARK EDGE

Published in 2017 by Dark Edge Press, an imprint of Usk River Publishing.

Usk River Publishing, Wales.

ISBN-13: 978-1520375885

Printed and bound by Usk River Publishing
Newport,
Wales.

PREVIOUS TITLES

Dedicated to survivors everywhere

What I Never Told You

Louise Mullins

The problem with secrets is they always find a way to resurface, usually when you're least expecting it. I've been keeping mine for thirty years. It's always been in the back of my mind, occasionally rearing its ugly head, but I thought I'd done a fairly good job of holding onto it. I certainly hadn't contemplated divulging it to anyone. I haven't spoken of it in so long that I'd almost managed to pretend it hadn't happened. Until today.

You're the first to hear it from me. No holds barred. In full 3D technicolour with trims. I warn you now it's not pretty. But I have to tell you because the police are coming. The one wearing boyish stubble disguised as a beard and the other one with the pale skin and chestnut eyes that always seem to hold a lingering gaze on me as though she knows what I'm thinking. Of course, she can't. Nobody can. I've always been rather adept at keeping quiet, as you'll come to learn.

I suppose you might think the way I've turned out has something to do with my upbringing or lack thereof, but you'd be wrong. I was a happy girl. Carefree. Gentle. Until that monster ruined it for me. Then I became a rebel. "Fuck the establishment" was my motto, and it got me further than I thought it would. Until those detectives showed up at my door.

I can see them parking the car up outside the house, making sure its locked before walking disdainfully up the garden path towards the front door. They glance at each other re-affirming what they have already decided to say, knowing I have no intention of hearing it. The female detective rings the bell expecting me to answer. But I don't. I was hoping they'd grow tired of their unanswered visits but they seem to be appearing more often in recent days, and I can't pretend I don't know why.

That's how I've come to realise that it's probably better for me if I told someone before they twist my words and make out that I'm not entirely innocent. Because nobody really is, are they?

There are two sides to every story, and I'm willing to give you the uncensored version, but it's up to you to decide which one of us is telling the truth.

DI SILVER

I'm leaning against a wall hidden from direct view of the porch. DI Locke stands, arms folded across her chest, eyeing the men on the opposite side of the street heaving furniture out of a van with suspicion. A nod to PC Watson, and we all turn towards the door.

It's a normal looking house. A terraced street lined with averagely affordable cars parked in front of the neat grey stone buildings which house a small easy to keep garden and a few potted plants.

Mr Wells' is flanked by two, slightly unkempt houses, cracks visible in the stonework, an architectural network of peeling paint and dry rot on wooden beams which accentuate the distressed roofs. Their gates rusted, and falling from hinges. A dog barks from somewhere nearby, sensing our early morning call as anything but usual in this typically quiet neighbourhood.

I lift the letterbox up and snap it back down several times before detecting movement inside the small home where our suspect resides. A shadow closes in towards the small frosted window of the front door. When it opens a woman's head appears, her body hidden from view, but I see the soft chenille fabric of a dressing gown in bright peach. She looks us up and down and pulls the door wide.

'What you doing 'ere?'

'DI Silver,' I say, holding out my ID card. 'This is my colleague DI Locke.' I nod towards Watson and the car, where PC Judd sits. 'You are?'

'Jacky.'

'We'd like to speak to Mr Antony Wells.'

'You'd better come in then.'

She leads us through a narrow hall and into a dusty living room where sheets have been used to cover the sofas. A pile of books litter one corner of the room, sat atop a curved edged table, the legs of which appear to be from another. The TV is on mute, but with the curtains drawn, it causes flashes of blue and green to streak the room. I don't sit, the room is cramped as it is. I can smell percolated coffee wafting in from the kitchen at the other end of the hall, which from here, I can see, sits a man, sipping his drink as though nothing is amiss.

'Police,' Jacky calls through to him.

The man looks right at me, places his cup down onto the rosewood dining table and stands, slowly edging his way down the hall.

Jacky beckons him inside and closes the living room door behind us. The room is hot and tight. The air fusty, The house is quiet. Too quiet. Why isn't he asking why we're here, or her, for that matter?

'Mr Wells?'

'That's me,' he says, triumphantly, as though he's won a prize. He's playing games with us already. Noted.

I give the nod to PC Watson, who pulls out a set of handcuffs from his trouser pocket and before Mr Wells gets the chance to complain, I move towards him so close I can smell the bullshit emanating from his BO laden clothes.

'Mr Wells, I'm arresting you on suspicion of obtaining indecent images of children. You do not have to say anything. But, it may harm your defence if you do not answer when questioned something you later rely on in court. Anything you do say can be given in evidence.'

He looks struck, as though he's genuinely shocked. I wouldn't put it past him if he *was* surprised. They all are. They never expect this day will come. They never think they'll get caught.

'I . . . I haven't . . .'

He walks alongside us, not protesting exactly, but making it clear that we've upset his morning ritual of coffee and toast.

'What's this about?' cries Jacky, whom I assume is his wife. 'Tony?'

An original nickname, I think, watching DI Locke pull the warrant out from the pocket of her coat, pressing it into one of Jacky's plump hands.

Water retention is a problem for her, I'm guessing.

Locke turns her attention to Jacky who's acting a little too calm for someone whose husband has just been arrested. 'Our colleagues will need to take a look around.'

'They won't find nout 'ere.'

'There's nothing for you to worry about then, is there?' she says, following me out of the door.

Inside the car, Watson on the passenger seat, me and Locke either side of Wells at the back, Judd driving, Wells looks down at his hands clasped together on his lap, thick hands, large enough to crush a child, and shakes his head.

'I haven't done anything,' he says.

I glance out of the window to see DI Blake and DI Flint, newly promoted, heading into the house, gloves on, ready to search the property. The sky is clear and the sun is already visible on the horizon. It's barely 8:00am by the time we pull up alongside the other vehicles in the forecourt of the central police station. I open the door and steer Wells towards the entrance to sign him in.

In the custody suite, he sits with his back to the camera, calculating how he's going to get himself out of this mess.

I turn my eyes from the camera to Locke. 'We've got him.'

Later, inside interview room five, below stairs, nowhere near the newly decorated hall, Wells seats himself down opposite DI Locke and I. I can tell the hour he spent thinking in the cell has done him some good because he stares at me wistfully as if trying to look past his afflictions, comforting himself in the knowledge he's done nothing wrong. And I'm sure, in his mind, he hasn't.

'For the purposes of the tape can you give me your name and date of birth?'

He takes a deep breath, then stutters, 'Antony Christopher Wells. The 8th of August 1967.'

'You've been accused of obtaining indecent images of children below the age of fourteen. Do you understand the seriousness of this allegation?'

The court approved solicitor who sits beside Wells passes him a handwritten note, telling him what to say.

'Yes.'

'One of our colleagues discovered a link to your IP address from a known source containing indent images of children.'

'I . . . I haven't done anything like that.'

'The images contain depictions of sexual abuse and rape against unwilling minors.'

He shakes his head and begins to tap his foot.'

'No.'

I lean over the desk. He folds his arms across his chest. A defensive posture that tells me he's hiding something.

'We have reason to believe that you have been ogling those pictures and playing those videos for some time, Mr Wells.'

'I don't know anything about it!'

'Your wife, Jacky, how are things there?'

'My wife?'

'How is your relationship?'

'Good.'

'And how are things in your intimate life, Mr Wells?'

'My . . . what?'

'Sex.'

'Sex?'

'No fantasies, fetishes, that kind of thing?'

'No.'

'You have children?'

'Hannah.'

I nod.

'And how are things with Hannah?'

'She's my daughter,' he smiles.

'Do you have any idea how those images and downloads appeared on your computer?'

'My computer?'

'I got the feeling you were expecting us, Mr Wells.

You didn't seem surprised when we came to your address?'

'I umm . . .'

'It's okay,' pipes up Mr Leonard, his solicitor. 'You don't have to say any more. Right?' he aims his question to me.

'Actually-'

'My client is struggling to comprehend this interview. I'd like his cognitive abilities looked into before we progress any further, detective.'

'As you wish. Is there anything you'd like to tell us before we conclude this interview and process your charge sheet?'

'I . . . my what?'

I sit back, slide the chair away from the desk and stand.

'Interview terminated at 10:28am.'

'Can I go?'

'That'll be all for now. My colleague will escort you to the front desk where you will be charged.'

Antony stands and makes his way towards the door, Mr Leonard at his heel like a puppy seeking approval. *Have I done you good?*

DI Locke opens the door a fraction to lead the men down the hall, and away from the smallest of the two basement cells that look dark and uninviting, though I doubt Antony noticed.

'I do hope our officers didn't leave your house in too much of a state, Mr Wells.'

That should rile him up.

'My house?'

'A warrant was issued during your arrest. Your laptop

and phone have been confiscated.'

'Can they take my things?' he says to Mr Leonard.

'Standard procedure. Innocent until proven guilty, isn't that right detective?' says Mr Leonard, offering me a cursive glance as he follows Mr Wells to the desk.

Locke turns to me and says, 'what do you think?'

'He knew what we were talking about.'

She nods her head faintly as if disagreeing with me.

'You don't think he did?'

'I can't decide. Something about his eyes. You know?'

I do know. I noticed it too. He can't look you in the eye when he speaks. Normally an obvious sign that someone is lying, but it could be an inability to articulate the seriousness of his charge. Or nerves.

'When will intelligence look into that laptop?'

'They're on it now.'

'Good. Let's see what they drag up.'

'Coffee?'

'Please. Make mine strong. I think I'm gonna need it.'

KATE

The knife glints in the sunlight filtering in through the locked window of the kitchen. I stand in front of the counter top, my eyes refusing to leave the blade. I reach out and feel the thick plastic handle, black against my pale hand with my fingers clenched tightly around it. Outside in one of the neighbouring gardens, I can hear children laughing. Their voices are being carried away by the roaring in my ears. I hold the knife for a moment, feeling the weight of it in my hand. My sight is muddied by the images that play on a loop, reeling along at such speed that I can't grasp at any one of them. The room is spinning and my vision clouded until I look up from the knife in my hand and see *him*.

His piercing blue eyes penetrate my own as if he can see straight through me and into my soul. The almond hair sprouting from his head, thinner now and greying. The creases around his mouth as he smiles turns my skin cold. The terror blossoms inside me and I feel as though I'm going to collapse. My heart is pounding in my chest, too fast, and my palms begin to sweat. The hand I'm using to hold the knife trembles around it.

I could do it. I could end this right now. Obliterate him from my life, from my head.

Everything around me has disintegrated. The room is a patchwork of fuzzy colours. The only object I can see with clarity is him. He steps towards me, his face betraying the threat of violence that fills the space between us.

My blood pumps quickly through my veins, flooding my skin with heat. My face prickles with sweat. My stomach churns and my feet refuse to allow me to back away from him.

He steps closer.

A scream lodges itself in my throat but seizes the moment I open my mouth.

His expression is one of confusion as though he cannot understand why I am frightened of him.

I look away from him and glance around the kitchen, catching sight of the door behind him. There is nowhere for me to go. Nowhere for me to hide. I am trapped, alone, with him.

My chest tightens as a fresh wave of panic rises up from my bowels and threatens to consume me.

He edges closer, forcing me back against the counter top. I can feel the ridges of the granite against my spine.

He smiles. The sickening, twisted curve of his mouth gives the impression he's taunting me.

I didn't mean to do it, but now the blood is everywhere.

I don't remember what happened next. I'm told that I raise the knife up in the air and lash out, lunging forward, stabbing it as hard as I can through the skin. The thick flesh breaks and I feel the knife hit something hard. Bone I think. The blood pumps out and sprays up the walls, some landing on my face and in my hair. It pours from the wound and drips onto the linoleum floor, leaving a pool at my feet. Some of it trickles down my arm.

His face pales in shock. He wasn't expecting that. He wasn't expecting me to fight back.

Now I hold the power. Now I'm in control.

I wrench the knife away. The blade is coated in blood.

I raise the knife again and as I'm about to strike out, the door behind him opens a fraction wider.

'Kate!'

I'm too lost in the moment to turn around and face him. Not now. I want this done.

'Kate, stop!'

An arm around my hand prevents me from being able to stab at the filthy bastard once more.

When I glance down and see Steven's hand clutching at me, stopping me from further violence I panic and drop the knife to the floor. His grip is strong, preventing me from reaching down and snatching it back up to finish what I'd started.

One hand presses down heavily on my shoulder and I feel myself being pulled forwards, one of his legs between mine, leaving me unable to run. He marches me out of the kitchen. I glance back at the mess I've left behind me, imagining *him* slumped over, clutching his chest, leaving my eyes fixed on his shape, but my head is swimming and the objects around me are blurred so I'm not sure if I've imagined seeing him lying in a pool of blood on the floor.

It's too late to save him. His life, as he knew it, has almost ended, but Steven is determined to save mine.

'Kate, what have you done? Why?' he says, his features displaying the shock that I felt at having been caught before I could complete my task.

How do I answer him? Words fail such actions, don't they? But if I were to tell him, I'd say that it's because I've had enough. That I can no longer live with it. That I can't go on pretending.

Steven hurries me along the hall, escorting me through the open doorway into the living room. He eases me onto the armchair facing the TV. I haven't the strength nor the energy to do otherwise. I'm worn. Mentally and physically exhausted. I'm tired from having spent years living with this beast inside me.

The monotonous tune of a car insurance advert fills my ears, drowning out the white noise in my head. I slump forward in the seat, but I don't crumble. I still have enough self-respect not to pity myself at having been caught in the act of ending someone's life.

As I sit there, my sight begins to clear. I can make out some of the shapes surrounding me; the sofa, the screen of the TV flashing, casting coloured light across the room. The curtains drawn. The pile of books in the corner. The objects becoming more familiar, more real. I cry out in anguish, at my careless actions, my awfulness, but I don't really feel anything. I can't. An empty void fills the pit of my stomach where the pain used to lie rotting me from the inside out. I glance down to my hands, held loosely at my sides, covered in blood.

I should feel anger at Steven for stopping me from ending it all; the lies and the secrets, but I don't. I'm numb.

He's standing in the doorway with the house phone pressed to his ear. His eyes won't leave me in case I jump up from the chair and run back to finish what I started.

'Ambulance,' he says.

He gives the call handler our names and address. The hot sticky air thickens around me as he tells them what has happened.

I consider running away from the house and leaving everything behind, but despite the rush of adrenaline still coursing through my body, I'm frozen to the seat of the armchair and I can't get my limbs to work though my head tells them to move. A fresh wave of panic fills me as I begin to realise what I've done. The consequences of my behaviour. And my chest tightens, my lungs constrict. I can't catch my breath.

I glance down again at my hands, the blood still dripping from my arm and down onto the floor and I feel nauseous. My heart continues to race and one thought forces my eyes towards the door where Steven stands, shaking.

I've made a huge mistake.

It's the same dream I've had many times, only tonight the memory is as sharp as ever. I awake to feel the familiar nausea creep up to my throat. Mornings like this stood over the sink retching, I think I might never be free of the nightly re-enactments of what happened to me all those years ago in that house.

Of course, the dreams have lessened in frequency, and have expanded and moulded into fictionalised versions of the truth. For one, I used the knife to slice my own skin, not *his*.

I don't believe in psychic ability, but when I think

about it now, it is eerily sinister that the night my unconscious brain came up with this scenario was the night before my life was tipped upside down on its axis, propelling me backwards, to a place I thought I'd long since left behind. Forcing me to acknowledge something I'd hoped to keep to myself until my dying day.

I suppose it's only right that I start at the beginning, or the beginning of the end if you prefer. I can't go back as far as when it all started. There are some things that the brain shuts off from completely, deeming it too difficult and dangerous to remember. But I can tell you that no matter how many events my mind has blocked from my consciousness, there are plenty it hasn't. All I can say for now is that I thought I was living the perfect life. I thought I was doing okay. Until I saw *his* face, bringing it all back; the fear, the anger, the guilt. And now I'm not so sure.

TERESA

I'd been in the garden for most of the day, tugging weeds out of the flowerbeds to stop them from strangling the budding plants any further. There was nothing out of the ordinary. The sky was powder blue and omnipresent. Everything was as it should be. I walked back inside the house to fetch the small trowel I used to dig up the most unruly of the weeds when the telephone rang. Its sharp shrill almost sent me backwards in fright, and when I answered it I almost wished it had. If I hadn't picked up the receiver I never would have known. But I did, and you can't turn back the clock; erase time or fix your mistakes as *Cher* had suggested.

Yes, I listen to music. I'm rather fond of the sounds of my youth; Elvis Presley, Roy Orbison, Jerry Lee Lewis and Patsy Cline. I used to enjoy listening to their soulful voices, lifting me up, reminding me of the day I fell in love, my first dance with a boy, my first kiss. The melodies bring it all back. It's all in there- the most important events of my life, running in sync through my mind as I drop the phone from my ear and let out a cry of pain for the devastating realisation that this could have all been prevented; this moment, this awful thing hanging over me may not have happened at all had I done things differently.

I am no longer, from this moment on, Teresa. I am the

mother of *that* man. The man accused of pouring over sickening images of children. Viewing the atrocious deeds others have committed to rip away every ounce of innocence from somebody's poor child.

I think of that girl then. Sophie. As I often do. I remember her face as though she is standing before me. Her crystal blue eyes and dainty features. She wanted to be a ballerina. I doubt she ever managed to fulfil her dream now that my suspicions have been realised. I know what happened to her. What my son did.

I feel as though my heart has been ripped from my chest and tossed to the floor where I lie in a heap, clutching the mini trowel to my stomach trying to gain the strength to stand.

I'm still lying on the carpet when someone starts knocking on the door. I fight the urge to remain here, let them stay out there all day if it suits them. Because I know what they're after. They want a piece of me. They want me to tell them things. Things I've kept to myself for thirty years. I suppose it's understandable really. They want somebody to blame. I am his mother after all. It was my job to take care of him, protect him. The trouble is, whilst I was focused on that I became blind to what was happening around me. And now the reporters want to know why I didn't stop him.

When I eventually gain the ability to move my limbs I find myself walking towards the door instead of away from it. I still don't know why, to this day, I didn't run. Why I didn't pack a bag, leave through the back door and into the garage to drive away- anywhere just to escape the vultures who stand in front of me, looking me up and down. But it's too late now. I stand in front of the house met with a bright sun and the flash of a camera lens on my face.

'Ms Carter, is it true that your son has been arrested for viewing child porn?'

'Did you know anything about your son's compulsion?'

'Could you tell us what your thoughts are regarding the offence he's been charged with?'

A woman with long auburn hair and kind eyes leaps in front of the reporter holding a Dictaphone in front of my chin. I'm about to reach out and snatch it from his long-fingered hand, but she shoves him aside and veers me back into the house.

It must have been the shock or the sudden impulse to hide that allowed her entry because I'm not the type of woman to let a stranger into my home. Especially a reporter.

She glances over my shoulder, noticing the wide open doorway into the living room and steers me towards the armchair. She tugs the curtains closed to block out the sight of camera flashes as photographs of my home are taken by wild-eyed wannabes, and enters the kitchen. I hear the kettle boil and the sound of a teaspoon clanking against one of my china cups. She returns to the living room pressing a cup of tea into my shaking hand and sits opposite me. I get the impression that she often makes herself at home in other people's houses, but I don't say anything.

She takes a sip from her cup and places it down onto the coffee table between us, looks me in the eye and says, 'my name is Rachel Harper. I'm an investigative journalist for *The Bristol Times.* I work on cases involving crime, and I'd like to hear your side of the story before anyone else decides to write anything untrue.'

She seems nice. Her voice is soft, sending me into a hypnotic trance. I feel like I'm coated in cotton wool. Numb. Her appearance is presentable. She's young but has obviously done this many times before. She seems genuinely interested in what I have to say.

'What makes you think that I want to talk to you?'

She glances around the living room as if to say, "well, you let me in." But she doesn't say this. She says, 'I'm interested only in facts. I don't print anything that can't be verified. But let's just say I have a personal interest in this kind of case.

I'm feeling less vulnerable now that she's divulged something personal. Though of course, I can't trust that anything she says isn't some form of entrapment, but I must admit I'm unable to imagine her hoping to ease me into a false sense of comfort before blabbing to her colleagues about the sad woman who lives with the knowledge that her son committed such an awful crime.

As if able to read my mind, she says, 'I'm freelance so nobody knows I'm here. I've got as long as it takes. But I need your permission before I write anything?'

I lean forward in my chair, contemplating telling her to fuck off. But I realise that now I have her here, there is every chance that she's telling me the truth. I can see it in the way she pulls a loose strand of hair away from her face and pushes it behind her ear. The way her eyes gaze at the floor, not quite looking me in the eye when she speaks about her interest in *this* case.

'Let's just say I had a difficult relationship with my

father.'

I take this to mean that somewhere deep down she understands the raw suffering that my son's actions have had on his fans, our local community, the entire country. But nobody, not even her, can possibly understand the pain a mother feels when her son is accused of *that*.

'Okay, but first I want you to answer a question of my own.'

She looks at me strangely then nods her head.

'What is your secret?'

She takes a few moments to decide whether or not to expose her darkest material to this woman seated in front of her, who has absolutely no intention of speaking to her if she can't open up and be completely honest as she wishes I to be.

She looks me straight in the eye and says, 'I had a drink problem. For ten years I was unable to get through a single day without alcohol. I used it as a crutch to forget something that happened to me as a child.'

'What changed?'

'I broke the silence. I sought help.'

And that is my defining moment. Because I knew all along I couldn't win by keeping quiet. Secrets always come out in the end.

That is why I decide to let her stay. To keep me company on my conversational journey back in time to a day that will stick with me forever because it was the pinnacle of my future. This bleak desolate landscape I can't quite see a way out of.

The day I gave birth to my son.

DI SILVER

Whilst Wells continues to plead his innocence, the media have other ideas. A tip off from one of the lower rank officers lead to a paparazzi blitz in the forecourt when I left the station yesterday. This morning it's quiet, but the murmurs that greet me from reception leave whispered words of uncertainty lingering in the back of my mind. Something I rarely experience. Despite four months of investigative work the case smells iffy.

'Did Sophie say why it took a media storm for her to come forward?'

Locke turns at my last comment and shakes her head.

'The seventies bred secrecy. She would have been scared,' she says.

'Maybe her parents didn't want to make a fuss?'

'No evidence they knew.'

'So she kept quiet all these years?'

'He has money, connections. People love his music.'

'Celebrity status syndrome.'

'Is that what they call it?'

'Fake it to make it?'

'More AA jargon?'

'Carry on as normal.'

She shrugs her shoulders.

'Sophie's a perfect example of what happens to a kid who's been abused. She's been in and out of rehab for the past fifteen years.'

'Box ticking?'

'Tetchy this morning.'

'I didn't sleep.'

'I won't ask why.'

There's no need. Everyone in the office knows about the divorce. It was a long time coming, I'll admit. Kez wanted kids. I didn't. It became the bitter fuel of many arguments added to by long working hours and a brief encounter with her accountant. She left me three weeks ago. I don't blame her for what she did, but I wish things had ended more amicably.

We weren't technically living together when she slept with Colin. We weren't even speaking. Our marriage had died long before him, but legally we were still wed, and now, we have to share the proceeds of the house.

'Have you found anywhere yet?' says Locke, unsure what my reaction might be at having been addressed to speak about my private life in the office.

'A studio flat on the Quay.'

'Bit pricey.'

'It's either that or out of Bristol.'

She eyes me with a look that says, 'you're happy with that?'

'I'll have enough to buy something local.'

'You're not considering promotion?'

'More paperwork?'

No, thank you.

'I take it you are?'

'I prefer to keep hands-on.'

I smile.

'So,' she says, 'intelligence had some interesting

things to say.'

'You've spoken to them already?'

She spins her revolving chair and slides it across the floor to where I sit, anxious to hear what they found.

'It seems Antony was lying.'

'Don't they all.'

'His phone,' she says.

'What have they got?'

'Images, videos and a few conversations.'

'He's been messaging girls?'

'For months. And, he's been talking to Sophie.'

'Interesting . . .'

'They've been Facebook friends since 2014.'

'And she never mentioned this?'

'Not in her statement, no. But I've just spoken to her and she says she was trying to elicit a confession.'

'The CPS are going to kick off about this.'

'I've sent everything over to you. Let me know what you think.'

I type in my password and enter the private email facility, downloading each file one at a time. Once I've finished I turn back to where Locke was seated, the chair now empty.

'She's with Dawson,' says DI Flint.

I leave the desk, cold coffee and incriminating files behind me, knocking lightly on the door.

'Guv.'

I look away from Dawson and nod to Locke, who looks as though she's been waiting for me to appear for some time. She has fire in her eyes, and if I didn't know better I'd think it was lust, but it's only a passion for the job that swims beneath those deep chestnut eyes.

'What do you think?' she says.

'I think we need to speak to Sophie.'

Dawson, hands face down on the polished black desk, nods his approval to continue.

'Find out what his wife has to say too.'

She doesn't say aloud what we're all thinking. That Jacky must have known about Antony's affairs. The late night parties. The strip clubs. The hardcore porn. The images of children and his conversations with Sophie, the woman who's accusing him of raping her at the age of seven. She must have known because it was all found on her phone.

'And the woman's parents, for that matter.'

'Sophie's?'

'Ask them why they left Bristol days after she's saying Wells abused her. Find out if they knew what had happened to her. And why Sophie was taken into care.'

'You think they knew, that they decided not to inform the police?'

'I'm saying, if you leave one stone unturned in this case, MOJ will be all over it.'

The Ministery Of Justice wouldn't bat an eyelid if the defendant were anyone else, but Antony isn't like anyone else. He's a gold mine of information that may lead to a few more arrestable suspects. We need him on-side.

'I think someone should tell Antony our plaintiff isn't to be trusted. Hook him up.'

'Then reel him in once he's grown complacent?' says Locke.

'Exactly. You've got seven days. Then I want him interviewed for the rape,' says the Super. 'Oh, and, try to keep your mouth shut.'

'What do you mean?' says Locke.

'Well thanks, to our informant, Wells is going to be headline news on the nationals tomorrow morning.'

'Great. That's all we need.'

It wasn't so bad when the reports were local, printed only in *The Bristol Times* newspaper, but of course, online, it'll be another sensation.

'A kick in the teeth is what it is.'

I know what the Super means. Every system in the country will be considered at fault for keeping quiet, despite nobody knowing a thing about it until drug-addled Sophie gave her rehabilitation counsellor Antony Wells' name during a therapy session. By law, she had to break confidentiality and inform us. Which just happened to be less than twenty-four hours after the news that Antony had been arrested and charged with obtaining indecent images of children.

'Maybe it will stir things up a bit.'

Perhaps others will come forward.

Outside, cigarette in hand, I turn to Locke as she slings her bag over her shoulder.

I lower my voice when I speak. 'Tut tut. Pulling a stunt like that.'

'I've no idea what you mean.'

'The press are going to be all over him. How is it going to look now he's been accused of rape?'

'They'll be less interested in why it took us so long to arrest him and more inclined to look into alternative avenues for sources.'

'His family?'

'Had a tip-off from Johnno. Turns out that Rachel Harper, the one involved in that missing student last year, has been given rights to the mother's story.'

'Now that's a turn-up for the books.'

She shakes her head. 'She might not know anything, but someone will. He's bound to have a few enemies. No-one gets that high on a pedestal without a little hostility.'

Or encouragement.

I follow Locke to her car, inconspicuous to passers-by that it's used to follow, search and arrest. Maroon red, the colour of the sofa I left to Kez, along with the rest of the furniture, which alone cost almost as much as the three-bed semi on Maple Road.

Locke stubs out her cigarette, tosses it to the concrete and gets inside the car.

'Belt up and don't look so glum. You're bound to find a place soon. The city is heaving with empty properties.'

'And blood-sucking landlords.'

KATE

The city heat is overwhelming. The sun beams down from a cloudless sky, and I curse as I step out of the car. I slam the door shut and belt across the lawn not paying attention to where my feet fall and snag the path that sits two inches too high from the pitted flower beds, centred in the front garden. Pain snatches my breath away and I freeze for a second before continuing towards the front door, limping. Our neighbour is watering the gardenia bushes at the front of her house. She raises her hand in a wave. She must have seen me stub my toe on the concrete path but she says nothing, just smiles.

I'm in too much agony to reciprocate so pretend I haven't seen her and shove my key in the lock, twisting it too hard so it bends. I step inside the cool house, slamming the front door behind me, and slump down to inspect the damage to my toe. There's nothing there. Not a spot of blood nor any other visible display of the searing pain that has left me speechless and hunched over on the bottom step of the wooden staircase.

I eventually manage to stand and drop the house keys on the countertop in the kitchen. Dumping my handbag on the large oak dining table, I fill the kettle and wait for it to boil. By the time I've taken a seat inside the cream painted living room and lifted the cup to my lips I can feel the stress of another busy day start to lift, my troubles slowly easing away. Tea is like a drug for me. I feel myself unwind slowly, like a cork leaving an expensive bottle of wine. I relax my shoulders and sink back into the armchair, breathing in the scent of the Ylang Ylang and lavender plug-in air freshener. The aroma reminding me instantly of visits to my grandmother who drank copious amounts of tea, needing it as much as oxygen.

It's been one of those hot days that leaves you irritated and breathless. It's lucky I was able to finish work on time, and for once I didn't hit the traffic. The heat gets to me. Damp skin makes me uncomfortable. Sweat is one of my weak points. Like shadows and enclosed spaces.

The heatwave that has lasted almost three days causes me to consider moving somewhere colder, damper. But this is England, it won't last long.

The sun makes my head itch, leaves my lips dry and causes my eyes to sting as I flick on the small fan that sits on the corner unit in front of a pile of books and root around the sofa for the TV remote. I find it hidden behind a cushion. I used to blame the children when it went missing, but now they've left home I know who is really at fault. The missing remote, a pile of crumbs on the kitchen floor, the empty toilet roll holder in the bathroom. It costs me almost as much time and energy to take care of my husband, Steven, as it ever did the children.

I switch on the TV and lift the cup of hot sweet tea to my lips but drop it the moment I see his face.

It's been years, but I'll never forget his oval shaped head, piercing blue eyes and almond coloured hair.

They're the first thing I see in the morning as I open my eyes and the last thing I see at night, though in recent years the constant reminders have abated somewhat they're still there lingering in the back of my mind like a bad smell.

Sitting here I'm suddenly forced back to a time in my life I thought I could finally leave behind.

I can't hear what the presenter is saying. I try to decipher the words by watching the way her mouth moves, but it's no good. Although I don't really want to hear it, another part of me needs to so I turn up the volume, the remote clenched tightly in my hand. When the news readers face is replaced with his once more, I jolt back into the armchair in fright as if by some miracle he will be able to leap out of the enlarged photograph on the screen and lunge for me.

'. . . arrested . . . come forward . . . sparking an investigation into . . .'

I switch the TV off and jump to my feet.

I leave the room with my heart thudding against my chest and my clothes soaked through with scolding hot tea. The cup lies smashed on the floor in front of the armchair where I'd been sitting moments ago when my world had been anchored firmly to the present. Now I feel like I'm falling; sinking into the abyss.

My limbs grow heavy as I make my way out of the living room. I make it towards the staircase before my legs give way and I collapse to the floor.

I clamber up from the floor quickly when I hear the front door opening. I can barely hold it together long enough to accept a quick kiss on the cheek from Steven as he glances towards my disheveled body to give me a rundown of his busy day at work. He doesn't notice the inner turmoil I've grown accustomed to hiding behind my weak smile and weary limbs.

I long to run upstairs and hide beneath the sheet on the bed, but I have to give the impression of being on top of things. Since my suicide attempt ten years ago, Steven notices any change in my mood and doesn't hesitate to pull me up on it. I move slowly past him as his arm brushes mine and flinch from the sensation of skin-on-skin contact. He stands in the living room, noticing the broken cup on the floor and the almost dried out puddle of tea.

How long had I passed out for?

I turn to make my way down the hall.

'You've spilt something?' he says, coming up behind me just as I enter the kitchen.

He doesn't wait for me to explain why I left it there for so long that the liquid has grown sticky in the heat. He eases me aside and pulls out the dustpan and brush from beneath the sink to tidy up the mess.

I grab a surface wipe from the cupboard beneath the sink and soak it under the hot tap, only realising I've burnt myself as he tugs it away from me, confusion written on his face.

'Didn't you feel that?' he says, turning to scoop the broken porcelain into the bin.

No, I want to say. I don't feel anything.

He leaves the kitchen to mop up the tea with a dishcloth and returns to rinse it out in the sink where I'm stood motionless, noticing the red marks on my hand where the boiling tap water has burned me.

'You look hot.'

My face is flushed with embarrassment. How could I have passed out from shock? Surely that's not normal?

'It's the weather,' I say, managing to act sane.

'I'm going upstairs for a shower.'

The idea of scorching hot water raining down on my skin overpowers all rational thought and I dive out of the kitchen and run up the stairs into the bathroom, slamming the door behind me just as Steven appears with a towel draped over one arm, hoping to wash away the stress of another busy day at work.

'Hey!' he says, jokingly.

I need a shower more than him. I need to rid the filth and grime from my skin. I need to scrub myself raw. I need to vanish the invisible hands I can feel pawing and clawing at my flesh, causing my stomach to tighten in knots of dread.

I leave the bathroom in a haze of steam, catching sight of my reflection in the full-length mirror as I enter the bedroom and sit on the edge of the bed. My pale skin is flushed and my hair lies wet against my face. I look as though I've aged in the hour it's been since seeing *his* face on the TV screen.

I wait for Steven to collect a clean pair of boxers from inside the dressing unit, taking it with him into the bathroom before I dare to remove the towel from my clammy flesh. I stare up at the set of rosary beads adorning the wall above the bed. Father Tom gave them to me at the end of the Christmas choir years ago. The children had sung their hearts out, proud that their mum and dad had made it. I'll never forget that day because it was their final year of primary school, and I'd been glad to kiss goodbye to the cliquey parents, allowing the kids to form their independence in secondary school. The beads remind me that I'd once believed in God. Something I haven't bothered to acknowledge since the children left home. Since I could no longer pretend to them that the world was a safe place.

Steven smiles warmly, finding humour in my lobster coloured skin.

'Didn't you want a cold shower? It's so hot out there.'

I can't find the strength to reciprocate his smile as he glances towards the window so I stand, giving him his cue to leave.

I don't usually mind him seeing me naked. But not today. Not after hearing *that*.

I drop the towel to the floor as I stand on giddy legs, my head swaying, wanting to dress as quickly as possible, slipping into a pair of leggings and a sports bra I use for the gym, before heading downstairs. Steven is on the phone, talking to one of the children as I scoot past him into the living room to switch off the TV. I don't want to catch another news report about *him*.

Lisa hasn't been to visit for a couple of weeks. She's busy with work at the restaurant she manages with her boyfriend Kyle. Dylan came over on Saturday with his wife, Ella, and my granddaughter, Skye. I begged them to change her name before she was twelve months old when by law you can do so, but they refused. I can't bear the thought of her being bullied when she starts school in September for being named after an object. What Dylan sees in these hippy ideals of Ella's baffles me, but I know she's a good mother and they're both happy so I keep my mouth shut to avoid any potential confrontation my honesty might cause. Which isn't unusual for me. I'm used to keeping silent.

Looking into the eyes of the man responsible for ruining my life all those years ago, was not something I had expected today.

I force myself to repeat his name aloud, trying to disempower him.

'Antony Wells.'

I hate you.

But I don't say that. I can't. Because hate is an emotion, like love or pity. And I feel nothing. He is as good as dead to me.

I've fantasised about killing him for years. In fact, for a while, after I'd married Steven and set up home, finally settling down into a normal relationship with a man I never thought I'd be capable of, I thought of nothing else.

I used to imagine shooting Antony, stabbing him, strangling him or smothering him in his sleep. Then I changed course and decided it was too risky to apply to the Avon and Somerset Constabulary for a gun licence. I stopped looking at knives, wondering how hard I'd have to pierce his flesh before he'd fall to the ground in a pool of blood. I wondered too how I'd ever get close enough to be able to wrap my hands around his throat and squeeze the life out of his ugly red neck. I finally decided to hold a pillow over his head until he ceased breathing, but that thought has intermittently been broken up with the image of a cell, somewhere I don't particularly want to end up so I'd all but given up fantasising about causing his death. Until now.

'Antony Wells, what have you done?'

Once the words have left my mouth, I'm not sure I can bear the answer. Despite not listening to the agonising details of the news report to hear the full extent of what he's been accused of, deep down I know what he has done. At least he's been caught.

I wonder who the woman accusing him of rape is. I wonder how she has managed to keep her mouth shut all these years and if the weight of the secret she had been carrying was as heavy as mine.

'It's all going to come tumbling out now, isn't it, Antony?'

I wonder if he ever thinks of me as he lies awake at night. Does he wonder what his life might have been like had he not met me? Does he even care enough to think back over his life at all? As I used to, night after night of endless obsessing, trying to analyse everything, hoping to find a new perspective. Evaluating what part I played in the demise of my own youth and which ones he did. Lying in bed listening to the wall clock ticking away the seconds, going over and over all the things I didn't do. Couldn't do. And trying to reason why.

I find myself stood at the top of the stairs. A wave of panic rises up from the pit of my stomach and I fall backwards in fright realising how clumsy and stupid I've been for not paying attention to where I'm going. I could easily have fallen down the stairs and broken my neck. At that thought the panic is replaced by something else. It grips my tightly, like a belt around my midsection. Longing. I long for some respite from my own fucking head.

I'm careful not to trip and fall, mindful of the dangers

that lurk within the walls of my home as I take the steps one at a time until I reach the bottom. They say more accidents happen behind closed doors than anywhere else. I think it's true for lots of things. Nobody really knows what goes on inside these walls. Like those I've built tall around myself, stopping anyone from getting close enough to hurt me.

I don't know why I'm thinking these things, but I know what re-ignited the low burning flame that had slowly begun to burn out through years of denial.

Antony Wells.

It's been thirty years.

I'm married now. I have two grown children who I managed to birth, raise and love without fucking them up. I have a career. I live in a relatively beautiful house. And I've finally discovered who I am. A wife, a mother, a carer. I won't allow anybody to strip me of those things. Enough has been taken from me. I was robbed of a normal childhood. I won't let anyone hurt me again. I'd kill them first.

I've always had a get-out-clause. It's been in the back of my mind for as long as I can remember. If it all gets too much: the lies, the secrets, the despair of what happened to me all those years ago, I could just end it. One act can rid the suffering.

Murder is a peculiar word. According to the dictionary, it means taking another living individual's life so, in effect, Antony has murdered me. So, if I killed him would that be classed as an act of retribution or revenge?

TERESA

Antony was a difficult child to love. From the moment he was born, kicking and screaming to get out of my womb he'd fought me past the line of patience. As I held him to my breast for the first time he struggled to break free and I wept in frustration. The midwife took him from me and fed him a bottle. He ate the lot then cried some more. In those early days, after the birth, I don't think I slept more than four hours.

The day we brought him home, exhausted from lack of sleep and numb from crying I dropped him on his head as I tried to change him on my knees. His scrawny little body had thrashed about so much that my hands couldn't reach out in time to catch him. He fell onto the hardwood floor. For a moment the crying stopped and he looked at me, right at me as if blaming me. Then he sobbed his heart out. I cradled him in my aching arms and tried to rock him gently to sleep, but his lungs continued to knock out that high pitched wail I didn't think I'd be able to get used to and he turned purple from the effort. He looked in that moment like a deformed plum.

I laid him in his cradle, desperate to rest my sore arms and put my feet up on the sofa to rid the throbbing pain in my stomach from carrying him around the room for so long, trying to shush him, and he almost instantly stopped screaming. When it happened again later, after another bottle - he still wouldn't take to my breast - I realised that he didn't like to be held and so in future I would have to feed him from a bottle, using formula instead of breast milk while he lay in his crib, propped up with a cushion.

He drank eight ounces of milk an hour throughout the day and every two hours during the night. I asked the health visitor one morning when she entered the house, clambering over unwashed piles of clothes and bibs if it was normal. To which she replied, 'you'll see when you have another one.'

I knew then that I never would. I couldn't go through that again. Though my mother begged me to give him a brother or sister, Christopher was happy to go along with whatever pleased me. He knew not to question my decision. He'd seen the vacant look in my eyes as I wept silently over the cradle, spilling tears onto Antony's head as he finally fell asleep, only to wake several minutes later with that high pitched wail I took to mean that he disliked living in this world with such a rotten mother as I, that I couldn't take care of two children on my own in the house all day. Not if they were both like that.

Christopher did his best. He took over some of the night feeds and drove the Silver Cross up the road to visit his parent's, to give me some space to think. But they always came back. I used to imagine an accident that left Antony in a coma or paralysed or something so that he'd stop crying and act like a normal baby, then I'd feel such immense guilt for thinking that way that I'd wake up from an almost trance-like state to find myself stood over his cot, his blanket gripped so tightly in my hands that they hurt.

My mother once said to me that Antony was a charm and would grow out of it. I prayed that it was true, but as the first year passed and he still hadn't learnt to crawl I took him to the doctor who told me that he was just a little bit delayed and would soon catch up with his peers. The developmental hurdles came and went and eventually aged three he'd learnt to walk and talk to the surprise of both Christopher and I. My mother said, 'see, I told you everything was alright. I've done this four times. I know what I'm talking about.' I didn't see the positive in her words, choosing instead to focus on the missing gaps in her little speech. What she really meant, of course, was that she was more experienced than me, and that experience came from having four children. Something that would never happen for me because I refused to sleep with Christopher from the moment Antony was born.

It didn't take him very long to find another woman to fulfil that role. I knew the moment Christopher stepped into the house with his eyes cast down and his lips pressed together trying to force the words he was about to say from breaking loose the moment he opened his mouth.

'I'm leaving you,' he said.

I was too tired to disagree with him. It seemed like a good idea under the circumstances. Though a part of me always assumed he'd return, he never did.

I was never close to my sister and my brother was in the army so we rarely saw one another. In rapid succession my mother died of cancer, my father distraught over her loss took to the bottle, and I rarely got to visit my siblings due to being left alone with Antony and his incessant crying which often left me bitter. Back then, I often regretted choosing to have him, wondering what my life might have been like had he died at birth.

DI SILVER

The smell of salt air, vinegar coated chips, and candyfloss emanate through the open car window. Gulls fly overhead, squawking in the heat.

'I still don't get it.'

'Locke looks over at me as she parks the car up alongside Sophie's parents' half-decent static caravan on the outskirts of Brean Sands, the seaside town I used to visit with my mum and dad as a child.

'Get what?'

'Why the mother never pushed for Sophie to get help.'

'There's no evidence to say that Sophie told her parents after it happened.'

'They upped and left their home rather quickly though, wouldn't you say?'

'Back then, those days . . .'

'No, it's more than that.'

She shakes her head. 'What?'

I look across at the grubby field surrounding us. The long grass in need of some TLC. The other static homes, plots built so close together you could smell each other's washing as it hung out to dry.

'They're travellers?'

'I didn't tell you because I wanted you to make your own mind up.'

'Why would I care?'

'Their culture is very different to ours.'

'Catholic?'

'That and, they move a lot. Maybe they were leaving anyway. Maybe it brought shame on their community, the thought that one of their own could have been traumatised by one of us.'

'Gorgers.'

I look away from the window, the sun-drenched field, the silent dogs, watching us, wearily. The men, shirts off to the wind, talking over a car with the bonnet lifted up.

'Is that . . .?'

'Stanley.'

If anyone were to know anything about Sophie, Stan would. Old-school, heavily built, loud, in and out of jail, but a loyal, hard-working son, husband, and father, he is the voice of the quiet South West district travelling community.

'I'll go and have a word.'

'Watch those dogs,' she says, her sarcasm hitting me square in the jaw.

Dog handler training, before I decided to apply to the sex crimes unit. Before I realised how challenging this line of work would be. I can't handle dogs. I learnt that the first day. They don't listen to me. I own fish. Tropical. Easier to maintain. Which is more than I can say for Stan who weaves through the long grass towards me, dipping his head in acknowledgement, two feral looking dogs at his feet.

'Wha' can I do for ya?'

'I'm looking for Mr and Mrs Anderson.' I nod towards the caravan that now appears empty.

'Gone. Took aff three days ago.'

'You've no idea where Sophie's parents are?'

'Na bother. Tea?'

I follow his cock-eyed walk through the dry yellowing grass, towards the sparkling caravan, Locke following along beside me. Stan's wife, Leah is inside wiping the surface of a mirror, still wearing the plastic see-through wrapping.

She nods once, switches on the kettle, and leaves us alone until it boils, returning only to pour tea into two china cups painted with filigree lace edges and adorning wildflowers, set between gold rimmed saucers. Replaceable but expensive.

'Thank you.'

'Ya welcome, Paul,' she says. 'It's been a while.'

I've learnt a thing or two about gypsies over the years. For one, they're not the hard-faced, violent type who think they're above the law that a certain television series likes to portray them as. They're decent, hardworking people, with a lot of love, holding onto long ago deceased traditions, who would do anything for their family. They're also loyal. Perhaps too loyal.

Stan Riley smiled and reiterated his honourable position as head traveller, leader, trust-keeper, and told me that he wouldn't talk about Sophie, whose parents had left the site three days prior. But he did give me some useful pointers as to why her mum and dad - if they were aware something had happened to her - might not have come forward about her abuse.

Catholic tradition asks you to forgive those who seek against you and offers salvation to those who've sinned. In a nutshell, her parents thought that denial would help them and Sophie to move on. It didn't work out very well. Sophie quickly fell from grace, slipping down the spiral of heroin addiction after a teenage pregnancy with a man ten years her senior, a gorger by all accounts, and has spent the past fifteen years in and out of drug detox and rehabilitation programmes.

'Feckin disgrace is wha' it is.'

I nod, sympathetic to Stan's words, noticing his gaze falling on a small pink jacket through the window of the shiny caravan to the field where his daughter, too young yet for school runs towards a ball one of the dogs has decided to bite through.

'We're doing everything we can.'

'I know. I know,' he says, as I stand, the shiny see-through film covering the pristine sofa sticking to my trousers.

'Thanks for the tea. Keep out of trouble.'

He waves me away and heads back to the car, now running, his brothers inside waiting for him.

As she presses the key into the ignition Locke turns to me and says, 'where now?'

'Let's pay a visit to the daughter.'

'Hannah Crawford?'

'Most men with a history abuse their own.'

'And if he didn't she might know something.'

'Exactly.'

KATE

I awake with a start. The sound of my heart thumping in my chest forces my eyes to snap open. The bed is damp with sweat. I turn my head on the pillow to see that Steven has already left for work. The alarm on my mobile phone hasn't rung out yet so I turn back to face the wall, closing my eyes hoping to find sleep again, but it doesn't come. I reluctantly get up and dress.

I make my way downstairs, wiping the sleep from my eyes, my head a foggy mess of memories mixing with reality at an alarming speed, causing my movements to become hurried and careless. I drop the first slice of toast I've made onto the floor and spill the coffee from the lip of the cup onto my T-shirt so I have to go back upstairs to change before returning to the kitchen in a panic as I realise the time.

I'm never late for work. Structure enables me to get on with things so I don't have to think. Steven says I'm always busy and that I need to slow down. When I'm forced to take annual leave I absorb myself in another world with a book so I can mentally play the part of a strong, independent woman taking on the bad guy in a thriller or fall in love with a handsome lord in a historical novel. Those stories give me hope that justice prevails and that good men exist. Until I met Steven, I never believed it to be true, but now my world has been tilted on its axis and I wonder if those books have even a hint of realism to them. Or do they just prolong the agony of denial?

The safety of routine and the typicality of my days has shifted for the first time in years and it doesn't sit well with me. I'm not sure you can ever be prepared for an event such as this one; someone from your past impeding on your present. No matter how much time I have spent trying to fill the void of my childhood with pointless exercises that leave me feeling just as hollow and as brittle as I felt back then. My old wounds have been re-opened and I've no idea how to sew them back up.

But I won't break. I am no longer that frightened little girl.

'Snap out of it, Kate,' I admonish myself.

I leave the house in a frantic speed, carrying a bin bag full to the brim of rotten food causing the stench to flood the kitchen, another reason for me to dislike the heat. The sun is hot on my face and neck as I lift the lid and dump the bag inside, trying not to breathe in. I make my way back inside the house to wash my hands before grabbing my handbag and keys and darting out of the door. As I'm locking up, I hear the familiar squeak of the rusted hinges as someone opens the gate. I turn expecting to see one of our neighbour's cats waltzing down the path searching for somewhere to poo, but come face-to-face with a rather odd looking couple instead.

The woman's heels clip-clop along the path as she turns towards the steps that lead to my front door. She has straight auburn hair, styled in a bob. It glistens in the sunlight. She's slight framed and wears a pair of marl grey slacks and a plum coloured short sleeved top. The man beside her wears a crisp baby blue shirt and a pair of black pressed trousers. His shoes glimmer with polish. They're dressed too fancy for Jehova's witnesses but too casual to be doorstep sellers.

They approach me without caution, the woman reaching into her coat pocket to retrieve an ID card. She looks self-assured, determined. I step back into the wall, scuffing my arm on the rough brickwork as the woman holds out the card to show me. My limbs grow rigid with fear.

'Mrs Lawton?'

'Yes.' My mouth is dry and my words come out staccato.

'I'm Detective Inspector Locke. This is my colleague DI Silver. We would like to speak to you regarding an ongoing investigation in which your name came up on our list of potential witnesses. Could we come inside?' she says, gesturing toward the door.

It takes a few moments to get my feet to move. My head is screaming at me to run, but my legs move cautiously as if I'm walking through treacle. I feel as though I'm going to pass out, but I manage to unlock and open the front door, leading the two detectives inside the house.

As the door closes behind me, I feel suddenly claustrophobic so I trundle into the living room and open the window wide, breathing in the stagnant air that offers little relief from the glaring heat of a bright sun.

I stand with my back to the window, inhaling to the count of three and exhaling to the count of five as quietly as possible.

When I gain enough breath to speak I say, 'how can I help you, detectives?'

I already think I know, but I want to give the impression of being unaware. I'm not giving them the satisfaction of disrupting my carefully composed life.

'Do you mind if we sit?' says DI Locke, glancing at the sofa.

I nod my head and stumble awkwardly as I sit opposite them.

They offer one another *the look* telling me their visit has nothing to do with home security since the recent break-in at number twenty-nine.

I think then that it might have something to do with Steven, who only an hour ago left for work.

'Is it my husband? There hasn't been an accident has there?'

DI Locke offers her colleague a cursory glance before focusing on me. Her gaze penetrates my skin, making me feel exposed. Vulnerable.

'Oh God!'

'Mrs Lawton-'

'Kate. You can call me Kate. Please, tell me what's happened?'

'Kate, we've charged a suspect as part of an inquiry into a historic case. During our preliminary investigation we came across your name as a potential witness. Whilst we cannot disclose any details to you regarding the individual who has come forward, we have reason to believe that you know the man we have arrested.'

I fight to catch my breath, feeling blood rise up into my cheeks.

'Wh . . . who?'

'His name is Antony Wells,' she says.

They both look at me, waiting for me to speak. When nothing comes, she continues in her monotone act of objectivity.

'We understand that you knew Mr Wells. You were close to him. In fact, you visited him often during the year of 1987.'

Though she is merely stating a fact I cannot help but wonder if her eyes betray the sincerity of her neutrality. Behind them I imagine that she is quizzing me, speculating that I might know something of use to them. Something that would help to build their case against him.

'1987? That was a long time ago.'

'Difficult to forget him, though.'

'Yes.'

'You remember?'

'Yes.'

'Would you agree to speak with us? It would really help if you could give us some more details regarding your relationship with Mr Wells. It would assist us with-'

'Your case?'

She nods.

'I'm sorry, but I don't think I can help you.'

The air in the room begins to choke me. Or is that guilt?

'It might help us to understand some of the timelines.'

'Help with inconsistencies, you mean? No.'

The word sounds hollow, but I mean it. I can't go through this again. I won't put myself in the position of potential ridicule and disbelief. Not if it means going over that time in more detail. It's in the past, where it must stay.

'You are not under caution.'

'You can't pressure me into speaking out.'

'I have no intention of doing so,' she says, glancing quickly to where her colleague sits nodding his head sympathetically.

I notice she's changed the *we* to *I*, perhaps with the intent of making a personal connection with me. Trying to build rapport. Trying to engage me. I'm not going to fall for it. I'm not going to crack.

'Get out of my house.'

For a second she appears crestfallen, but stands, and makes her way to the door, her colleague following along behind her. I hold the door open waiting for them to exit when DI Locke turns to me and says, 'if you wish to discuss something you remember, you can contact me here,' handing me a business card as though she's a florist or a local artist and not a detective wanting me to give away my darkest, ugliest secrets.

'I won't.'

I close the door behind them, sink to the floor, and curl into a ball to sob. Just as I did as a child, hours after being robbed of my dignity. My innocence.

I've been fighting away the tears since I saw Antony's face on the TV, but now it's finally sinking in that life as I knew it is once again being swept from under me.

I was expecting the police to visit when I heard of his arrest, but I didn't think they'd be here asking questions so soon. I haven't had enough time to prepare myself for this eventuality. I haven't even got my story straight.

I force myself up from the floor when I notice the

time. It's too late to call in sick, but I can't go into work red-eyed and despondent.

I've been a carer since I left my position at the bookshop which went into administration during the spark of the recession. People don't read paperbacks these days. They prefer those Kindle things I can't get used to. My own has been sat in a cupboard since Steven brought it home for me as a surprise. 'You can store thousands on there,' he said, not understanding the look of distaste that swept across my features. How could he know the joy of pressing your face into a crisp hardback copy of a long-awaited title to inhale the wonderful aroma of new pages when he hasn't read in years?

An image of Steven's disappointed face comes to me then. The concern breaking his confident features as I tell him what dark secrets I've kept from him, as I wipe away the tears before picking up the phone. I have to inform my boss that I won't be coming into the office today. I can't face anybody right now. Steven would be devastated if I told him. I need some time to get my act together.

Ms Smythes will miss me terribly. We've developed a bond that can't be broken. She reminds me of my late grandmother with her war stories and devout Catholic rituals. Always with her head in the bible as I enter her small property on the outskirts of Filton. Today is her bath day and she refuses any other carer the responsibility. Her morning will be shaken up and she won't know what to do with herself. The agency worker they'll have to call in to take over my shift won't know how Ms Smythes likes to read a scripture before her bath. How she takes her morning cup of tea (with cream instead of milk in a bone china cup). The agency staff cost money and the home care company will have to skimp on supplies this week: gloves and pens. The more I think about how my absence will affect those poor men and women who rely on me the more I find myself convinced that my absence would be selfish and disastrous. Then the boss, Todd Moresham, answers the phone.

'It's Kate, I'm running late. I'm so sorry, can you let Ms Smythes know. I don't want her to worry?'

'No problem. Get here as soon as you can,' he says before hanging up.

Relief washes over me and I finally manage to force myself upstairs to smooth down my hair and re-apply the black liner to my wet eyes. I don't want anyone to think I can't cope with the challenges of my job. Work is the only respite I get from my head.

I make it into work almost an hour late, but manage to get to Mr Rogers' house at breakneck speed without having to play catch up. He's easy to care for. All I have to do is bring him the newspapers that arrive daily through the letterbox and make sure he takes his tablets with a short glass of sherry.

He made me promise not to disclose his little morning drink to anyone, and I agreed it was probably for the best. He's not supposed to take alcohol with his tablets, but, as he said, he doesn't have long before God ferries him away, and I'd rather he died happy. He doesn't like to think of himself as a burden. Something I have to repeat daily is that it's my job to look after him. The only burden he carries is his own belief that he's in the way. He laughs then, a throaty cackle that often leads him to choke on his own breath.

He's been living with lung cancer for five years, but it hasn't taken him yet. I admire his ability to enjoy what little time he has left. And it seems he has more than most. I discovered an expensive packet of cigars in his bedside cabinet two weeks ago when he asked me to fetch him a clean pair of socks. One of them had been smoked halfway down to the butt. Today, another sits in his bedside table at least two inches shorter. I smile warmly as I close the drawer and pray that his lungs take him through the rest of the year. He's looking forward to spending Christmas with his daughter in Wales.

I have two more morning visits before I can stop in at Greggs for a short lunch break. I drive down the Gloucester Road, parking up on one of the side streets nearest the small coffee shop on the corner.

I take a seat at the window, overlooking the busy street, feeling re-energised from work. I open the newspaper as I take a large sip of coffee. The waitress brings over the custard slice I ordered, places it down onto the table with a smile and walks away. I look down at the open paper, the headline jolting me back into my chair. It takes every effort I have not to jump up from my seat and flee as the words pinch at my resolve. My vision blurs, the page now crumpled in my hand. I force myself to gulp back some of the hot coffee and stuff the custard slice into a napkin to eat later if I can stomach it. I can't eat now.

I leave the coffee shop and stand rooted to the pavement watching the world spin around me. Everyone is concerned with their own activities. I step aside to avoid being hit with a French stick jutting from the carrier bag a woman holds as she shuffles past, narrowly avoiding walking into the toddler who sits in a buggy with his little fat legs poking out of the sides, trying to kick people as his mother pushes him along the pavement.

I have the sudden urge to scream. To alert the woman to pay better attention to her child. To the cars passing by to be more alert of pedestrians who chance the road, avoiding the extra ten foot walk to the zebra crossing. Don't they realise how fragile life is? How one moment of error can alter your life forever? One careless mistake and your life could be over. I want to shout at them, to warn them. Of course, I don't, they'd think I was a lunatic. And, even if I managed to find the courage to tell them the words would freeze as soon as they reached my tongue. I have been silent for too long.

I return to the car and drive towards Miss Gill's. A polite, petite woman with a love of foxes I've never been able to comprehend. Her cottage in Westbury is decorated with thousands of them. They sit on the mantelpiece, are used as door stops, and cover the walls. She even wears a T-shirt printed with a large fox across her stomach. She doesn't say much but is always very appreciative of our time together, making sure I stay long enough to finish a cup of tea. I disappear into the bathroom - the caffeine overload taking over my bladder - before I leave, hoping the reprieve from instigating conversation will clear my head long enough to stop the rising panic.

I finish my shift an hour later, having left Miss Riley, a big, brash Irish woman in her garden. I'm not sure what to do with her, she doesn't need any domestic help, but I get the impression she values the company so I don't tell the team. Loneliness is a killer. I saw a documentary about it once; the amount of elderly people living in Britain today with no family or friends to visit, spending days, often weeks without holding a conversation with another human being. It begs the question as to what lives my clients would lead if there was nobody to visit them. I dread to think.

I make it home without hitting the evening traffic. Steven is standing in the porch, speaking to someone on the phone, the front door wide open to the heat. My stomach tightens when I see a shadow cross his face. I wonder if he's speaking to the detective. Has DI Locke called to tell me something she'd forgotten? I try to think of something to say to Steven when he questions me, but I needn't have worried. As it turns out, it's his brother Charlie. I know who he's talking to as soon as I step out of the car and overhear him discussing football results and fishing licence prices.

A few hours ago I felt like a simmering wreck and now I feel normal again. It's amazing what a busy workload can do for you. I don't understand these women who give up their jobs to stay at home all day, despite their children being in school. What do they do with their time? What could I have done with mine?

I kick off my shoes and sit back in the armchair as Steven approaches, dropping the phone in its sleeve on the shelf behind me.

'Dylan and Ella are coming over,' he says, as if I need reminding.

I can't wait for Skye to come barging in, recounting her day at nursery through breathless lips, and charging through the house like a bat from hell. They used to visit every Wednesday until their jobs began to take up more and more of their time. And now, it seems we rarely get the chance to catch up. I'm looking forward to the house being filled with noise, but not her mother's insistence on covering the tops of the doorframes with rosemary to ward of negative vibes. I need the distraction.

I notice Steven has bought a copy of today's newspaper. The *Bristol Times* lies folded in half on the coffee table, unread. I've forgotten about my earlier glance at the article in the coffee shop, remembering only as I stare at the front page, Antony's face leering back at me. Aged fifty, a volunteer minibus driver for the local school where he lives in Bedminster.

He doesn't look as though he's aged, but I suppose, to me, he will always be the man who changed my view of the world from believing it to be bright and full of opportunities to realising that it is overshadowed with darkness.

At the age of thirteen, I felt invincible. I was a shy, self-absorbed but carefree girl, popular at school and awaiting my first kiss. Fast-forward two years and I was an angry, rebellious woman with a "fuck you" attitude and a hideous nose ring that made me look like a bull. The aim of which, however, was not to put the boys off my slight figure and newly formed breasts, but the men.

TERESA

I spent the first three years of Antony's life trying to get to know him, to no avail. It seemed he was unable to grasp the most basic of social etiquette. He didn't even try to communicate with me, it was always one sided. Though I guess it helped that all he had to do was gesture with his hands and I was able to understand what he wanted without the need for words. He couldn't express distress, and instead cried at the slightest thing: the whirring of the washing machine, the sound of the post sliding through the letterbox and falling onto the mat, next doors dog barking as a motorbike screeched down the road. Everything seemed to unsettle him. I thought he might have acquired my mother's nervous disposition, but it was more than that. I knew it, but nobody else seemed to notice.

One day I managed to coax him away from the cardboard box he liked to play with, putting his toy duck into it then taking it out, over and over again. We made it to the local toddler group upstairs in the church hall of the Horfield Methodist on Churchways Avenue. He wouldn't hold my hand, but neither would he leave me to go and play with any of the other children. One of the mothers from the group came and sat beside me and handed me a cup of warm sweet tea. He looked up at her as if to say, 'you can't take my place,' then walked slowly away. She asked me about Antony and told me all about her son, the same age, slimmer, red haired with an almost translucent complexion. The things she said got lost on me as my eyes remained focused on Antony who seemed fascinated with pulling the legs off a doll that a little girl had left on the floor beside him. When my mind returned to the conversation I caught the word *different* and glanced at her. 'Your son is so calm, so self-assured. Don't you think?'

'You said different?'

'Yes, they all have their own quirky unique ways. Your Antony seems far away. Like an angel sent from above.'

If only she knew, I thought, before a loud choking sob began to sound from somewhere nearby.

I turned to see Antony crying his eyes out over the coat a woman had slung on the back of a chair right where he was standing. I could see the fear and anguish on his face even from where I sat but I had the sudden urge to run instead of hold him in my arms and try, without success, to calm him.

I knew then that the difference between all the other mothers and I was that my son hated me. He didn't want to be here. He didn't ask to come. I'd forced him from his neat ordered life where all he wanted to do was sit on the floor and play with his stupid box. I'd let him down. I couldn't get out of there fast enough. With him kicking, screaming and attempting to wriggle from my arms, I was afraid I'd drop him onto the concrete outside so I made him walk, dragging him home with tears in my eyes and a heavy heart.

He quietened the moment we reached the front door

and he sped through the hall and into the living room, taking a seat on the floor in front of his box.

Angry and hurt that I couldn't even share a few precious moments with my son without his hysterical crying fits taking over the event I decided I'd had enough. I snatched the box up off the floor and tore it into shreds, tossing it into the garden to place in the bin later, when I'd have hopefully, finally, managed to get him to stay in his cot to sleep.

I didn't think at the time that what I was doing was cruel in any way. I just had to get rid of that damn box and all it represented: his oddly strange behaviours. I thought that if I continued to play along with his bizarre rituals I'd only be enabling them to expand and grow worse. The thing is, at the time, I had no idea that the suffering it would cause was going to contribute to his behaviour. I'd not heard of developmental psychology back then. I had no idea that I was going to create a monster. If I had then I would never have kept him. I'd have given him away the moment he was born.

I once read an article in a magazine about a woman who'd become psychotic since the birth of her son. She'd become convinced that he was a changeling. A gift from the devil. I thought back on that first year of Antony's life and saw some of the similarities between her story and my own. I'd been warned about the baby blues, but I suspect that I'd suffered some form of post-natal depression. Perhaps somewhere on the psychosis spectrum. There was a day I remember vividly, when so distracted, tired and tearful, I'd actually thought Antony was an alien and considered drowning him to ensure the mother ship wouldn't make me keep him. So convinced was I that this small child, who didn't seem to share my DNA, belonged to someone else that I even considered calling the hospital to check he hadn't been accidentally swapped after birth with another similar looking child in the maternity ward of Southmead hospital.

Of course, I never told anyone about those beliefs. Which is very well because they were so fleeting that I'd almost forgotten them. Until today. When I started looking back, checking if the signs were there, and I'd missed them. Wondering if there was one particular moment that turned my son into the evil man the media claims he became.

DI SILVER

'What do you think of Kate, then?'

'She's scared.'

'You don't think there's any more to it?'

'Are you always so suspicious?'

'Of everyone I'm afraid. It's part and parcel of the job. But, on a serious note, didn't you get the impression she was holding something back, rather than being frightened of speaking out?'

'Maybe.'

I saw the photographs of her children. I noticed her husband's coat in the hall. She had a comfortable home. But she didn't look content to me. Behind her eyes, I saw anger.

'I don't think it's fear. I think she's in denial.'

Locke continues the drive without comment, but I can sense the hostility radiating off her. She thinks I'm getting too involved. Again.

Back inside the office, there's another development awaiting my attention as I pour over emails and case files seeking a reason to coax the CPS into charging Wells for Sophie's rape. It seems that her case could be compromised by her decision to invite Antony into discussing their shared childhood. A friendship she claims was one-sided.

Entrapment.

The phone records show that Sophie instigated discussing her rape with him on at least eleven occasions.

Locke appears at my side, breaking the monotony of pouring over files that make my hands feel dirty. 'I've got the CPS on the phone.'

I head towards her desk, press the phone to my ear and prepare to be told that the case isn't going to trial.

'As you know, the MG3 doesn't hold enough evidential material to prosecute Mr Wells with rape.'

What she means is there's no forensic evidence.

'Yes.'

'My colleague, however, has just been informed by the Met that another woman has come forward, claiming Wells attacked her around nineteen years after Sophie alleges being raped.'

'Has she given a statement?'

'Indeed.'

I take the woman's name and notice Locke's unwavering gaze grow increasingly inquisitive.

'What is it?' she says, as I put the phone down and turn my attention to the lemon sponge cake she's planted in front of her.

'The media coverage has done its job.'

'I told you someone would bite.'

Locke grabs her bag and hurries to the door. I'm a few feet behind her as I leave the station, stepping out into the blazing sun.

KATE

I wave to Skye as she trundles down the path, taking Ella's hand and looking up to her father with glee. I suppose she's high as a kite on the sugared doughnuts I made sure she ate, despite her mother's protestations that the bean salad she had for lunch was enough to fill her until dessert, which will probably entail a basic fruit salad. I don't wish to remind Ella that Skye's diet could do with a healthy dose of fat to build up her thin legs, but I wish she'd see the hidden intent behind my ploughing her with cakes and ice cream every time they visit. After all isn't that what grandmothers are supposed to do?

Steven offers me a plate, piled high with the buffet food left-over from our little tea party. It's something we used to do when Dylan and Lisa were small. We've continued the ritual so that once a week we don't have to cook. I stare at the plate of food, willing myself to eat.

I'm not hungry. I haven't cooked anything in two days. Having sworn off meat, I usually manage a garden salad, some fish or a couple of curried vegetable burgers and couscous, but not today. Nor yesterday. Not since those detectives came to visit. Their visit has dampened my appetite even more than seeing Antony's face in the newspaper. Unable to bear a morsel of food touching my mouth I cringe at the sight. It revolts me.

'Are you alright?' says Steven, eyeing my plate.

I nod my head, not daring to answer in case it all comes tumbling out. I haven't spoken of those things in years, but the way I'm feeling right now, I might just crack and let it all spill from my lips.

I gaze into his ignorant eyes and feel a pang of regret at having never told him. He has absolutely no idea about my past. I've never hinted at it. There never seemed to be the right time. During our courtship I wanted to forget about it. Once we were married I felt as though it would be too soon to broach the subject. After Lisa was born, I thought it was too late. And so, it's never been spoken about. I've kept quiet all these years because I didn't want to upset him. I didn't want to rock the boat on our loving journey together. But now, I'm not so sure. Perhaps I should have been straight with him right from the start. My chest tightens with self-disgust. I don't deserve him. I've been dishonest with him for the entirety of our marriage.

But then, if I did open up, how would I begin such a conversation?

Steven is my rock. He's safe. He's secure. Others might think he's boring, but his solidity grounds me to the present. Would speaking of it now do more harm than good? Would it shatter his depiction of me as the controlled, capable woman he fell in love with? Would he wonder what other things I'd kept from him?

You hear about those things almost daily. In the newspapers, in magazines, on the TV. You see the anguish and hurt secrets like mine cause once they're awoken from their sleepy vigils. I couldn't bear to speak about those things to Steven. I couldn't say what damage leaving those images to replay in his head might cause. I'm used to it. I've lived with it for thirty years. He has never known such sadness, such desperation, such terror. An emotional pain so raw that it almost physically hurts.

'How is your food?' he says.

I look down to my plate and begin to dig around it with my fork. Miniature pastries and mini pizzas sit aside cocktail sausages and cheese straws. I squirm as I place one into my mouth.

'It's good,' I lie.

It's awful. I feel like a fraud. Like a useless, worthless nothing. A speck of dirt. A piece of shit.

I shiver.

No. Don't start that again, I tell myself. Stop thinking. But . . .

And so the internal battle resumes.

I can't sit here any longer, pretending that everything is fine when all I want to do is hurl the plate across the room and watch it shatter into tiny pieces, spraying the wall and floor with food.

I leave the chair and make my way over to the sink, filling a clean glass with ice cold water from the decanter on the fridge.

'What's wrong?' says Steven, leaving the table to come and stand behind me. His warm hands press lightly against my hips, manoeuvring me towards him. I want to break free from his touch and run upstairs. I want to fall onto the large comfy bed and close my eyes to sleep off this nightmare that haunts me, but I know that even when I do manage to fall asleep, Antony will fill my dreams. He's in my head and he won't get out.

'I'm fine. Just tired.'

There is only one way to get rid of him. I have to face up to this. Perhaps, if I understood the reasons behind his behaviour, I might be able to come to terms with what caused him to act the way he did towards me. Denial, though it had previously been my saviour, no longer appears to be working.

'Go upstairs and have a rest. I'll bring your food up later.'

'Okay.'

I pull away from Steven, leaving his hands to fall down by his sides as I make my way upstairs.

I stand in the bedroom gazing out of the window overlooking the street where two small children play tag in their front garden. There's a paddling pool placed right beside the small wall separating the garden from the pavement. I want to shout out of the window for the parents to send their children inside. Don't they realise how dangerous it is to leave children unsupervised at the front of the house?

I tried not to smother Lisa or Dylan. I tried, but failed miserably. I didn't want to be one of those over-protective mothers who waits around at birthday parties and doesn't allow their children to attend sleep-overs, but some part of me couldn't accept that there was an alternative. That my children, if left to develop a healthy independence would blossom into well-functioning adults with a healthy attachment to their own children. I tried to keep them from harm, and look what that achieved? I have a daughter who lives a hundred miles away in London, and a son who can't settle down in one job for too long, who relies on his wife far too much. Just like he did with his mother. I've created two children who couldn't be more different to my perfect ideal because of my own past. My own problems.

The children across the road have been called inside by their mother who hovers in the doorway waiting for her son to clamber down from the tree at the end of the garden nearest the three-foot high wall where anyone could reach up from the pavement and snatch him. I shake my head and try not to feel anger at her stupidity, but holding it in only causes me to shake with fury.

I'm sitting on the edge of the bed listening to the ticking clock. It's monotonous clicking a metronome to my thudding heartbeat. I attempt some breathing exercises I learnt at the Adult Education Centre. It was a short course in meditation. I only went to fix the boredom that came with waving Dylan off to his new life with his new wife, but it taught me how to control my breathing and to calm my nerves whenever they became too much. Though what good it does now I couldn't say, because the harder I try to stop the panic, the more difficult it becomes to tame.

Other things I've found helpful, aside from keeping busy are the repetitive actions of polishing, vacuuming or speed-walking. Sometimes just taking the car out for a long drive is enough to settle my thoughts, but I'm not sure I'd trust myself behind the wheel today. I might careen off the road and slam the car into a wall just to see if I can do so and still make it out alive. To test the strength of my own mortality. To check with God if I still deserve to live after what I've done. Or not done, should I say.

In a way, I'm an accessory, aren't I? By keeping quiet I've enabled that monster to continue to hurt others. I'm as guilty as Antony.

Though I appear to function there's always been a part of me that fears others seeing what goes on behind my eyes. There has always been a part of me that desperately clings onto things to hold down the growing sense of dread at the thought of losing control. A deep rooted fear that one day someone will find out who I really am: a fake. I used to think that should Steven ever discover my secret he would leave me to run off and shack up with some tart from his job as a health and safety officer.

Does anyone else feel this way? This constant sense of impending doom? As if one day their entire world is going to be tipped on its head, that they'll fall to pieces?

Steven appears in the doorway. He brings the plate of food with him and rests it on the bedside cabinet. When I glance at the clock I realise it's been almost an hour since I came upstairs.

'Are you sure you're okay, you seem . . . distant?'

'I'm fine. I've just got a headache.'

He sits beside me, resting his arm against my back, letting me know without words that he is there for me, always. My chest tightens and my stomach knots up when he places one palm face down on my thigh. I try to still the waves of anxiety that creep down my arms. I focus on his wedding ring, a symbol of our commitment to stay together, to love one another, until the end, and I try to relax my muscles. I yawn. He falls for my feigned tiredness and stands, bending down to kiss my forehead.

'I love you.'

'I love you too.'

He hovers beside me for a moment.

'You would tell me if there was something bothering you, wouldn't you? You know you can talk to me about anything.'

'I know.'

But not this.

'You'll be okay? Do you want anything?'

'No, I'm fine. Really.'

He holds out his hand to entwine my fingers through his, a silent offer of support.

'I'm going to lie down for a while.'

He smiles, releases my hand and walks towards the door. I wait until he's gone before removing any of my clothes.

The weather is still hot and sticky so I decide to wear a thin cotton nightie to bed. I stare down at my legs and feel exposed the minute I put it on so dive beneath the sheet we've been using to sleep with since the heatwave began. It lies on top of the duvet and when I lift it up to cover my face, I feel instantly better. I can hide away from the world and pretend that I'm invisible.

I lie there for several minutes, trying to block out the negative thoughts that whirr through my skull, springing out at me like jagged pieces of rock if I give them power. The sheet that cloaks me feels heavy. The air in the room is thick and humid. Everything around me begins to tighten, constricting my breath like hands across my throat. The weight Antony's shadow has cast over me is suffocating.

I crumple the sheet between my fists and bite down hard on the cotton to stop myself from crying.

Antony doesn't deserve any more of my tears.

When my anger is spent I tug the sheet away,

satisfied with the pain I feel at having gripped the sheet so tight.

I look at the plate of food Steven left beside me and a wave of hunger rips through me like a bubbling sickness that won't leave until I fill the emptiness that burns in my stomach like fire. The void I usually fill with work, cleaning and reading now requires me to consume copious amounts of pastry. I grab a handful of food and cram it into my mouth, chomping wildly, not tasting it as I swallow it down in gulps. Then I stare at the empty plate.

'You fat bitch.'

I walk towards the bookcase, thumbing the paperbacks stacked neatly together in order of author and genre, but nothing sparks my interest. I don't think I'll be able to concentrate on anything anyway. What good does filling your head with another's issues do, really, apart from act as a form of relief from your own troubles? It used to work, but my head is too jumbled for that crap now.

I know I'm losing it, my ability to function. For the first time since I left counselling in that small converted town house, twenty-five years ago, I feel as though I'm floating on the water of a great ocean, waiting for the waves to pull me under and swallow me.

I snatch the business card DI Locke gave to me from my handbag and flip it over and over in my hand, feeling the smooth texture of its shiny surface. Reading her telephone number once, memorising it straight away. A photographic memory does have its perks, but most of the time it frustrates me. I only have to experience something once and the entire episode can be retrieved in full technicolour details from then on, and not always when I want to remember it. It's a blessing as well as a curse.

I put the card down. Pick it back up. And continue the action once more before sitting back down on the bed, the card gripped tightly in my shaking palm.

I wonder who made the complaint. I wonder what she told them. Am I repeating the same actions she did by flicking the card over and over in my hand, considering speaking to the detective? Did the woman who came forward perform this very task? Did she break the silence for her own ends, to secure justice for what happened to her or did she wish to ensure Antony couldn't hurt another girl? Were her experiences as horrific as mine?

I pick the phone up from its sleeve, agonising over whether or not to call the detective, wondering what I will say if she answers. I go over the implications of doing so, wondering what questions will be asked. I think of all the things I haven't had the courage to tell Steven in twenty years of marriage. Things I haven't spoken about since I walked out of my counsellor's consulting room at the age of twenty-four, saying goodbye to my past for what I thought would be the last time.

I've moved on with my life since then, haven't I? I'm no longer that battered, broken woman I was back then. Talking about it doesn't make the pain any less raw. But the wound I thought had almost healed is now weeping, and I'm scared it will become infected. Maybe I should confront it. Perhaps I should speak to DI Locke if only to discover what her true motive is because I know she has one. They always do.

Whatever she thinks she knows is nowhere near the truth. She has no idea how difficult it is to break free of the binds my abuser has over me. She wants my evidence to secure a conviction. She wants to use me. She came here trying to portray a ray of hope by offering me the chance to make peace with my past, but really she wants to send Antony to the gallows. The only question is, will I let her?

I wonder how awful jail is for someone like him.

My brain does not compute my movements. I act as though my body has been taken over by another entity.

What possesses me to dial DI Locke's mobile number, I can't say. I still haven't decided what to say when she picks up, so on the third ring I panic and end the call. I wait a few minutes with my finger rested lightly over the redial button before trying again.

The same thing happens.

I breathe in and out at the count of three, lengthening each inhalation and extending the time between each exhalation to the count of five then ten as I've been practicing for years until I've calmed myself enough to redial. I end the call and go through the same motions once more, vowing this time to wait until I hear her voice before I consider ending the call.

I dial once more, with the phone held in the crook of my neck, and sit on my hands to stop myself from ending the call as soon as she picks up.

This time I hear her voice.

'Detective Inspector Locke speaking. Can I help you?'

I don't know what to say. I didn't think this part through. I open my mouth to speak but the words freeze in my throat.

She repeats her name and adds 'is there anybody there?'

After several seconds that feel like minutes I finally find my voice.

'Kate. It's Kate Lawton.'

'Hello Kate. How can I help you?'

'I don't know . . . I'm not sure what . . .'

'Take your time,' she says.

'I don't know how to . . . what to say.'

'There's no rush.'

I hear the softness of her voice. Her gentle tone, warm, empathic, engaging, willing to hear the words that I can't quite assemble let alone voice. Despite the determined way she greeted me yesterday morning, today she seems to have all the time in the world.

'I'm ready.'

That's all I can say. I'm ready to talk. I don't know what use my involvement will be to their case or what will happen from this moment on, but I know that I have to do this. I don't know why, I just do. I can't contain the guilt I feel inside that has wedged itself in my chest like a disease. A cancerous tumor that will grow and spread and fuck up everything I hold dear. Just as it almost did as I crammed pills into my mouth before slicing my wrists with a vegetable knife.

The silence eats away at you, tainting everything. As painful and awful as it might be, I have to stand by this woman, whoever she is, who has taken the courageous step to come forward and speak out about what Antony did to her. I have to if only to free my own conscience.

What that vile monster did to me has tarred every

thought, every action, every decision I've ever made. And I know that if I don't do this I will be as guilty as Antony is for pretending those things hadn't happened.

'I'm ready to talk.'

Some part of me always knew that one day I would say those words, but it doesn't make them any easier to voice. In fact, I feel worse, knowing that this woman, this stranger, this detective is going to want to know everything. Every sordid detail. Every dark twisted thing I endured.

'This is a big step you've taken today.'

She says this as if to reassure me that I can change my mind now. I can put the phone down and return to my old life. A life filled with questions, of masking my fears of the dark, confined spaces, crowds and of being alone with only my thoughts for company. I can go on keeping on, but what has that achieved so far? A nice house, a decent car, a husband who I've kept in the dark all these years?

My mind has never been at peace. Memories of that rotten time in my life all those years ago have left a deep-rooted bruise on not only my childhood but my every waking moment.

I no longer want to keep quiet.

I'm doing this for her, the unknown woman who is braver than me because she instigated this whole thing. I am doing this for myself so that I no longer have to fill my time with constant activities. I'm doing this for Antony, to give him the chance to redeem himself, to tell the truth, to suffer. I'm doing this for us, for men, women, and children everywhere who don't have a voice, who can't speak out, who are too afraid to disclose their darkest secrets. I'm doing this for humanity.

'What happens now?'

'I'd like to meet with you to discuss things. If there's anything you can tell us that might be useful for proceedings we may wish to take a statement.'

There is a beat of silence before I manage to mumble, 'okay.'

'Are you free tomorrow?'

TERESA

Antony's first day of school was filled with a mixture of horror, dread, and relief. It was a daily battle to get him to complete even the most basic of tasks, like wash, dress, comb his hair and eat, but it was a tragic compromise for me to get rid of him for half the day. No matter how bad his behaviour was I had to push on through despite it because he was my son. And because he was all I had. Suddenly without him by my side I didn't know what to do with myself.

My father fell over drunk one night, hitting his head. He never recovered from the brain damage and died in hospital several weeks later. My sister had married and moved away, starting her own family and my brother had decided to retire from the army aged twenty-four and met a young woman whilst abroad. He wrote to me a few times telling me how wonderful and hot it was in Italy with the woman he'd decided to make a new life with. I tried to be glad for him, for all of them and tried not to dwell on the past but it was hard.

Antony reminded me every day of his father. Of what we once shared, and what I'd lost. And yet in so many ways Antony was obviously different. For one, he had almond coloured hair that grew in waves. Christopher's had been dark and straight. Mine was lighter and curly so I assumed he'd stolen some of my genes, after all, as well as my sanity, though it was difficult to tell what else he'd inherited from me. Certainly not my temperament. I learnt that early on. Whereas Christopher was placid until provoked I resumed a more passive attitude when it came to displaying my emotions when under immense strain. Which if I'm honest, was most of the time during those early years of Antony's life.

After his first day of school, Antony grew quiet and moody. Irritable when I needed to be alone and distant when we were together. I assumed he resented me for abandoning him, but when I asked him what was wrong he just moaned about the noise inside his head and the bright strip lights of the classroom, covering his ears at the memory.

I tried taking him out with me for walks in the park or shopping, but avoided it as much as possible. The effort of having to explain his oddly demanding behaviour and incessant rituals was difficult in itself, but what irked me more was having to explain why my son had to walk backwards out of a shop as we were leaving because he'd walked forwards coming in or had decided not to go to school today and began screaming at the top of his lungs so that I had to carry his large-boned body all the way home, despite him being five years old.

I had been convinced by my mother, his teachers, and the health visitor that his behaviour was normal and that he'd grow out of it, but when a mother from the school playground had invited me round for tea one afternoon before walking with me to collect Antony and her son Tim from school I realised there was definitely something wrong with Antony. I could no longer deny it.

Whilst Joan spotted Tim walking towards her at the

school gates, I noticed the way he held her gaze, came towards her for a hug and smiled up at her before he began to recount his day at school. I glanced down at Antony who stared straight ahead, eyes focused on something across the road before he darted out of the school gates and leapt towards an oncoming vehicle in order to reach the cat who'd perched on a nearby wall on the other side of the street. He had no sense of danger, no common sense when it came to traffic. No moral judgement. He didn't even see me as I grabbed the collar of his school shirt, hauling him to safety. He blinked once as if to say, 'what did you do that for?' but he didn't speak. He just continued on his way down the pavement towards home not looking back, not caring if I was following him or not.

As soon as we came through the door of the house I turned him towards me and he listened to me with eyes darting around the room as I tried to instill in him the seriousness of his actions.

'You could have got yourself killed. Didn't you see the car? Don't you know not to run off like that?'

He didn't answer me.

I was too angry to attempt to explain to him the dangers of crossing roads so I did the only thing I knew would work. I locked him in his bedroom for the remainder of the evening, until it grew dark and cold and I knew he'd be hungry.

He didn't even bother to ask me why he was being punished as I opened the bedroom door to release him some hours later. It was as if nothing could touch him. That's when I realised that it wasn't that he didn't understand emotions, but rather he seemed to lack them.

There was a hot Summer afternoon once, when my father was still alive when we'd walked to the park for a picnic. My father had made sandwiches, and we ate sponge cake beneath the shade of a willow tree in the centre of The Downs. It was hot so I'd layered tons of suncream on Antony's pale skin. He didn't even seem to be aware of my touch.

As we packed away our things I turned to see Antony heading towards a fallen tree stump. Beside it there were several large stones and rocks. He picked one of them up and threw it as hard as he could towards his grandfather. I was too stunned to say anything, realising it had just missed my father's head by a couple of inches. Antony could have killed him, but when I stopped him and leant down on bent knees to explain the dangerousness of what he'd done, he stood there, blank faced listening, but not really engaging with the words.

I went ballistic. My father was too shocked and so relieved not have been seriously injured that he remained quiet for the rest of our journey home. All the while, Antony seemed unfazed by the incident as though he'd already forgotten it had happened.

That was the first time I can remember looking at my son not with contempt or regret at having birthed him, but with genuine fear for his future. If he couldn't see the harm in his actions, where would they lead him?

DI SILVER

When I finally hear the words I've been waiting for, the seven-day grace period is almost up. It's Friday. I'm about to leave the office to compile some paperwork for an attempted rape on a man who met his assailant in one of the nightclubs in Old Market last Saturday. The CPS are reluctant to agree to charge the man whose victim consented to sex before passing out in a drink and Ketamine-fuelled sleep in which his "date" took advantage.

We have a second witness to the Wells case.

When Alex Thorne speaks, I almost fall off my chair.

'You can officially charge Mr Wells with two counts of a Section 1 Rape,' says the Crown Prosecutor, I'd all but assumed should swap her role for defence.

Wells will remain in his cell on remand at Her Majesty's Pleasure Ashfield, granted a thin blanket, weak tea I'm sure the prison officer with the beard spat in, awaiting the inevitable beatings from the other inmates whose privileges allow them internet access until a trial date is given. Why the government allows paedophiles and rapists to view photographs of bikini-clad women and children's adverts in between rented Netflix videos I can't answer.

When I call the prison, 'he's staring at the ceiling,' is the latest update from petite Sandra, who swapped her role as Police Support Officer for the downgraded uniform of a PO in order to spend more time with her family. An ex-work colleague and very good friend. 'Right headcase he is. Just sits there mumbling to himself. He's got a mental health assessment in the morning.'

Another thing they all do is plead insanity or child abuse caused their warped impulses. I'm not falling for it, and by the sound of it, neither is she.

The magistrates hearing for Sophie's claim was straightforward. Section 1 rape of the Sexual Offences Act 2003. The problem we have now is that to secure a conviction there has to be a host of required assessments carried out, including Dr Cotes' psychological report. If he wants to, Wells could use this to bide his time. The longer he's on remand, the less time he'll get at sentencing. They all try this one on too.

'Fancy a drink?' says Locke, as I'm leaving the office later.

'I'm gonna get changed first.'

She waits beside Lynne, the reception clerk, booking in another offender for obtaining indecent images of children, all boys under the age of five.

I've grown a thick skin in this job, which is just as well because I need a thick liver too if I'm going to match Locke drink for drink.

'There's a darts match on tonight at the Llandogger.'

'I'm not going anywhere near that place,' she says, remembering being pounced on by some drunk who thought she was his sister's friend.

It's hard not to view everyone through a lens, giving people a certain typology by their looks, choice of clothing, job or lack thereof. It took me a while to see the differences, their gait, body language, history. It's why I wonder, as I head into the crowded lounge of the backstreet pub opposite the Wharf with Locke at my heel, why Wells takes pleasure in hurting innocent girls.

It must have something to do with his own early life experiences.

KATE

I make my way into the suite with a heavy heart. Knowing that there is every chance that speaking to the detective might not lead to anything.

The suite is decorated in muted tones of cream and beige. I sit on a plastic chair in front of a camera which if I were giving a statement would record every agonising detail as I recount my story. But it remains switched off. DI Locke tells me this as if recounting a fairytale, but what I have to say is far from pretty.

I haven't slept more than six hours in the past two nights. I've been given sick leave and my rota has been given to Tracy until I return to work. I'm over-tired and can barely get my thoughts together as they scramble about inside my head, let alone find the words to speak.

I inch back in the chair, pressing the heels of my shoes into the navy blue carpet to ground myself.

DI Locke takes a seat on the small soft chair in the warm, homely, sparsely decorated room that bears the scars of other's unfortunate experiences.

'Are you ready?'

I nod once, not trusting what might escape my lips if I am to speak.

I haven't spoken of Antony for years. I'd put those moments in a box and buried it at the back of my mind. Compartmentalising my past into small, sharp fragments

I had no intention of piecing back together. I focus my gaze on a thread coming loose in the carpet, trying to silence the negative words - 'keep your mouth shut,' 'you're going to die' - undulating through my skull.

The detective places a lined statement sheet on her lap and holds the pen upright, ready.

'You know Antony Wells?'

'Yes.'

'You spent a lot of time with him when you were younger?'

'I did.'

'Could you tell me about that?'

'He used to play in a band. I was into that kind of music. Punk Rock.'

'How old were you?'

'Fourteen.'

I swallow hard.

I breathe out and open my mouth to speak, but once again find the words caught in my throat.

'It's okay,' she says, waiting for me to start. After a few moments, she says, 'how did you meet him?'

'It was Summer. Like this, hot and sticky . . .'

I leave the suite over an hour later. DI Locke listened intently, barely speaking as I recounted the day I met Antony and the friendship I thought we shared over the following two years. I left out the horror and pain. I'm not sure why what I wore was important to her, but she asked lots of questions about my clothes and the music I liked. It sent me back to that Indian Summer in 1987 when my childhood was ripped away from me before I had the chance to figure out who I was.

I spent years afterwards trying to develop my own identity, but always, at the back of my mind, I felt tarnished.

Violated.

TERESA

When Antony was seven we went camping in Woolacombe Bay. The drive was as torturous as the unrelenting sun that cast a constant misty haze across the landscape, and rain thrummed against the car windscreen. We made it unharmed four and a half hours after leaving the small house I'd started renting using the small monthly payment Christopher paid towards Antony's care. It wasn't much but it was enough to move somewhere quieter where Antony could feel at peace. It was also more isolating for me, though I tried to make the best of it.

I had to do one big weekly shop, aided by Grace, a kindly neighbour who took a fondness to Antony right away. She lived at one end of the street in Westbury, and we used to meet for tea and cake every Thursday. She worked the rest of the week as a secretary. I'd managed to find myself a part-time seamstress position in a launderette on the Gloucester Road by then, but it was only a matter of time before my boss, a stout pot-bellied man with a temper and no patience for what he called "idleness" would release me of my duties. I knew I wouldn't be able to keep the job for long when I was asked to attend another school meeting about Antony's unruly behaviour, and had to explain to my boss that he was ill, justifying Antony's behaviour as something real and medically fitting. Bus travel was expensive in the sixties so I used to walk a lot, which often caused me to be late collecting Antony from school.

My legs were still killing me as I parked the car up on a sloping hill, overlooking a pub just as the rain began to spit down at us. Tired from having driven the longest journey I'd ever taken since passing my test, - having been left my father's car after his death, and not wanting to let it go despite its rust and difficult manoeuvring, - I managed to keep it running for almost five years before it finally packed up on me.

The holiday itself gently lifted me from my troubles. Just being away from home and the stagnant air that filled the space between me and Antony as I drove one hundred miles to the campsite, left me feeling desperate for conversation. The steady beat of music emanating from the pub doorway where a man stood in the darkness with a lit cigarette in hand beckoned me. I couldn't keep my eyes off the dark brooding stranger. My senses prickled, having been dampened for years by dirty nappies, violent tantrums, and Antony's needy temperament.

'Come on,' I said. 'We can pack our things into the caravan later. Let's go and get a drink.'

Antony reluctantly followed behind. The pull of an alcoholic beverage was too much to ignore. I was on holiday and I wanted to enjoy myself.

The sun had set long before we left the cramped little pub and said goodbye to the landlord, who it turned out had a son, close to my age. I was twenty-seven then and I like to think I had a classy air about me that didn't require a man to ply me with alcohol to find him even vaguely attractive. But Geoff, the landlord's son, and handsome mysterious stranger I'd seen shadowed in the doorway seemed honourable.

When we returned to the car in a howling wind, escorted by Geoff who assisted us with leveraging our suitcases from the boot of the car and into the dusty, shabby little caravan, that at the time was all we could afford - having managed to get a good deal from one of the mothers at the school whose husband owned it - I settled Antony down on the sofa that folded out as a bed and left him alone with some pencils and a pad of paper that Geoff had found whilst clearing up one of the more modern caravans at the other end of the campsite. It had taken almost an hour to settle Antony because the wind, like rain, made him anxious and howl like a demonic wolf with fright.

As we settled down with a glass of whiskey Geoff found during one of the clean-ups that morning on his rounds he told me that he knew of another child like Antony. I never asked him what he meant because in the heat of the moment, tipsy and free of the constraints of life back in Bristol, I kissed him. I also wanted to stop thinking and talking about Antony. This holiday was as much for I if not him, and I didn't want to hear my son's name. In that moment, all I wanted was to be held.

Geoff smelt of cigarettes and grass. Being a groundsman, I took it as a given part of the job to smell like the earth he worked on all day. I let him take me outside and across the green where his own small abode sat nestled between two large sycamore trees, leaving Antony asleep, alone in the caravan.

We made love in the light of the moon that cast a blue

glow onto his face. I joked that he looked like a martian which was when he told me about his hobby. He said he liked to gaze at the stars and spent many nights looking up at the sky to where nobody and nothing could touch him. I found it fascinating in my slightly drunken state.

We spent almost every evening of the holiday together, walking along the beach, drinking in the pub, and of course, having sex. But when it came to our last night, I realised what a terrible mistake I'd made letting him into our lives.

Antony was asleep. It was late and whilst I was tired I'd been looking forward to saying a final goodbye to Geoff in the only way I knew how. Ours wasn't a holiday romance. It wasn't even close. We both needed companionship, I more than he, and knowing that we would never see each other again made that night all the more special. Until it was ruined.

I allowed Geoff to lead me into the curtained off area where I slept, just metres away from Antony. We made mad, passionate love, and this time I didn't hold back. I let myself sigh aloud and moan and rock against him with pleasure. Only, as our bodies melted together, something caught my eye. A shadow, barely visible in the blackness of the half-used field fell across the make-shift bed. I closed my eyes, telling myself that it was a trick of the light or a swaying tree branch in the distance. Perhaps it was a cat creeping along the ground outside, its shadow making it appear as though it was inside the caravan, but when I opened the curtains I saw Antony staring at me through the darkness. I jumped up in fright, almost headbutting Geoff as I flung the bedcovers away from me and charged towards Antony.

I was appalled that my son had seen me naked. Embarrassed and ashamed, I reached out to where he stood and demanded to know why he was still staring at the fold out sofa I'd just left, but he didn't flinch.

He was still looking at Geoff's naked half-covered form. He didn't seem to find anything wrong with what he saw.

DI SILVER

I follow Locke to the door, but for the third time this week Ms Teresa Carter doesn't answer.

'She's scared.'

'Or avoiding us.'

'She can't avoid the case. It's all over the news.'

Locke darts me an unconvinced look.

'All right. She doesn't want anything to disturb her life, but you can't deny something like that. It isn't healthy.'

'Therapist are you now?'

'The Chief's signed me up on a psychology diploma.'

'Ah-ha, so that's where your recent concern with offenders criminal trajectory's come from.'

'So what.'

'I didn't have you down as the type to be interested in Pavlov and Freud.'

'It's not like that. Look, most sex offenders begin their criminal careers young. They start by shoplifting which leads to car theft, then burglary, assault . . . They rarely commit their first rape as a teenager.'

'You're saying you think there are more women?'

I nod.

'Another thing, how did he keep off-radar all this time?'

'Money?'

'He could have paid them off, but I doubt he's sold many records in the past few years.'

'Maybe that's why he's broke.'

'Maybe.'

'I get it, I really do, but that doesn't explain why he did it. Wells' learning difficulties, his strained relationship with his parents, isn't that a more likely cause?'

'That's what everyone thinks, but there's no evidence that he was abused.'

'That's not what I'm saying. I think his MO has something to do with his mother.'

'Not daddy issues then?'

'You watch too much NCIS.'

'You read too much.'

I can't help smiling. She has a point.

'We'll try again later.'

We pass a couple of reporters lingering on the pavement as we leave.

The curtain twitches and I glance towards the window to see the faint outline of a woman I recognise.

'I swear I just saw that Rachel Harper in there.'

'Really?' Locke looks stunned.

'Maybe Teresa does have something to say about her son, after all.'

KATE

It's difficult to express how I'm feeling right now. I'm relieved that it's over, but my skin itches with guilt and self-disgust. I recounted as much as I could without implicating myself. I couldn't give a shit what happens to Antony, but I've no intention of speaking out in a court full of people so I had to withhold anything that might suggest I was abused in that house. My skin feels dirty and I'm looking forward to a hot shower.

I walk back to the car, parked in the multistorey, glide onto the seat, close the door to the world and close my eyes.

'It's done. It's over.'

I grip the steering wheel tightly, releasing it, then again three times to calm my trembling hands before pulling away.

As I reach the traffic lights I come to the conclusion that I'm kidding myself by pretending that it's over because really this is just another beginning. There is no end to the inner turmoil I feel. If there was, surely I'd have found it by now.

'Leave the police to do their job.'

It's out of my hands.

I travel home on automatic pilot as if my movements are being acted out by someone else. Numb from the waist down.

'Stop thinking,' I say, as if the words will somehow reach the dark areas of my brain and stop me from remembering.

As I pull the car up alongside the house and inch my way out of the vehicle a ton of lead has fallen on my limbs making my movements sluggish; my bones heavy with the weight of the things I never said.

Steven greets me in the hall carrying a plate stacked with sandwiches, his face beaming.

I smile back, unfeeling.

'How was your day?' he says, taking a seat beside me in the living room, leaving a trail of crumbs to fall down his chin and onto his shirt.

'The usual.'

He pauses for a moment, before adding, 'have you got something on your mind? It's just that you don't seem yourself at the moment.'

'I'm fine. I'm just tired.'

He places his hand on my thigh and I immediately startle from his touch.

'You're jumpy.'

I want to make sure that bastard is getting sent down for a very long time before I open up those old wounds and share them with Steven. I don't want to ruin what we have.

'I'm just tired and achy. I think I might go upstairs and lie down for a bit.'

He nods, unsure.

I rub my hand over his bald spot as I stand.

'If you need to talk to me about anything, I'm right here,' he says. 'I'm not going anywhere.'

Maybe not yet.

'I know.'

'Good,' he says, laying a light slap on my backside as I turn and walk out of the room, heading upstairs.

There have been times when I've needed him. Like after the miscarriage, the little girl we should have had between Lisa and Dylan. Emotionally he has always been there for me. But I don't expect him to support me through this. I don't want to involve him. This is my problem and I have to deal with it alone. He can't possibly understand what I've been through, I wouldn't want him to. Having the both of us upset and worried isn't going to do either of us any good.

I close the bedroom door behind me and sink down onto the bare mattress. I lie there staring, counting the dips in the knotted pattern of the ceiling rose. I notice a cobweb in one corner of the faux crystal chandelier and I'm instantly thrown back into the past. The turmoil that followed what happened in that cold, soulless room. The belief that what happened was my fault.

I swallow back the bile that wedges itself in my throat, turn over onto my side and weep silently into the pillow.

It was him.

Antony.

He ruined my childhood.

Half an hour passes before I gain the strength to haul myself up from the damp duvet and drag myself downstairs, painting on a glacial smile that could break at any moment. Fake it to make it, as I was taught in school. I can't remember who said it now. It was a long time ago. The Catholic secondary run by nuns devoted a lot of their time to instilling in us the value of politeness, kindness, and forgiveness. But I never believed in that. Not after . . .

I enter the living room and curl up beside Steven on the sofa, half-listening to the TV programme, my mind elsewhere, knowing that my world could be shaken at any moment, and this, this tranquility between us is just another lie wrapped around us like a fishing net.

It's the calm before the storm.

Steven switches channels and I stare vacantly at the screen before realising that I haven't eaten.

'Got any sandwiches left?'

Steven passes me the last cut from his plate and watches me with steady concentration as I nibble away at the bread until it's gone.

'I know what's troubling you,' he says.

I blush at the thought of him knowing anything. The way he looks at me convinces me that he saw me driving away from the witness suite. Then I imagine he overheard my telephone conversation with the detective.

'You're on one of those fad diets again, aren't you?'

'No,' I say, the tight knot in my stomach dissolving.

'You get moody when you're dieting.'

'I'm not dieting.'

'Then what is it? What's wrong? I know when something is troubling you. We've been married long enough for me to notice the signs.'

'Nothing is wrong with me. Give it a rest.'

'I'm your husband, you can't keep anything from me,' he says in a mocking tone. But I know he's worried. I see the concern written in his eyes.

I look away, unable to hold his gaze.

He's right. I have got something on my mind. I am

eating less, but not because I'm on a diet. But because every morsel of food that enters my mouth reminds me of the sexual acts I was forced to perform, and the guilt I feel for not stopping it makes me feel too sick to eat.

'You're my world, Kate. If something is troubling you, I have a right to know.'

I glance up as he leaves the sofa, collecting the empty plate from my lap, heading towards the kitchen.

'Steven, I'm fine. It's-'

The shrill of my mobile impedes on our conversation.

Saved by the drill I think as I offer him a weak smile and pull the phone from my handbag.

I recognise DI Locke's number straight away.

'It's work,' I say, moving across the room towards the french windows.

I step into the evening heat, closing the patio doors behind me, and turning away from Steven's inquiring gaze.

A knock on the window alarms me and I drop the phone on the grass, glancing up to see him making faces through the window, his breath leaving streaks across the glass.

I stifle a laugh, pressing the phone to my ear and shooing him away.

He grins and darts off into the kitchen as DI Locke begins to speak.

TERESA

Antony was a placid child when he wasn't howling at the moon or trying to describe something utterly pointless that seemed to enrage him. After a difficult few years, he seemed to outgrow his need for the comfort of my presence and began walking the streets late at night, like a cat prowling for prey.

I called him in one evening as it was getting late, and as he walked towards me I saw that he held something in his hand.

'Sleeping,' he said.

It was dead.

I picked the bird up from the ground and tossed it over the wall into the lane.

After supper, I went upstairs to switch the light off in his room to find Antony hunched over something, whispering into the darkness.

'I know you didn't mean to scare me, but it was wrong and you had to be punished.'

Where he got those words from, I'd no idea. I'd never used the word *punishment* despite having to utilise it frequently to disable his wild mood swings. I didn't see how locking my son in his bedroom when he'd done something wrong like bitten a child in school or pinched a packet of sweets from the newsagents down the road could harm him. I never beat him or shouted at him. It was the only way I knew how to control him.

'What are you doing with that bird?'

I raised my voice an octave when I saw that it was in fact, the dead one he'd brought back with him earlier.

'Did you kill it?'

He looked at me with confusion, unable to string enough words together to comfort me.

'It flew at me.'

'So you killed it?'

'I wanted to keep it in my coat so it couldn't fly at me again.'

'You smothered it. You held it too tightly.'

He just shrugged.

I left the room to fetch some toilet roll and wrapped it up. I took it out of the house through the back door and deposited it on the ground at the end of the garden. I turned around and my breath caught in my throat when I saw Antony stood in the doorway staring at me with the neutral expression I'd come to understand meant that nothing I said entered his thick little skull.

He saw no wrong in anything he said or did because he didn't care. That's what I'd come to realise. It wasn't that he lacked the ability to construct emotions. He wasn't an imbecile. He just didn't care for anyone but himself.

'You are a selfish little bastard and I wish I'd never given birth to you.'

I didn't mean to say the words, they just slipped out. But they didn't even seem to sting him.

He turned back to the house and went upstairs to his bedroom. I didn't bother saying goodnight. I didn't want to look at him.

I curled up on my bed and tried to sleep but images of his fat little fingers wrapped around that poor dead bird punished no doubt for flying too low, too close to him, sent shivers down my spine.

What was becoming of my son?

DI SILVER

The sexual offences act committed on a person under eighteen is usually a straightforward case, but Antony, of course, is pleading not guilty. Meaning Sophie will have to testify in court against the man she claims raped her. One positive is the third witness, Isla. A foreign national who lives in London. A high-class call girl. A woman who has a long list of clientele from top end actors to sportsmen. As with most victims, her right to anonymity permits her to say what she pleases regarding the accused because the public will never know the truth about the awful crimes committed against her. But this case is quite different to Sophie's. Isla claims to be his most recent victim, alleging to have been raped by Antony in 1996 when his career spiked after a reboot of punk style music, something I've never understood the joy of listening to.

Due to the unfortunate hostility of the Met, we are forced to watch her interview recording via video link.

'I was . . . how you say? Working.'

'As an escort?'

'Yar.'

'And where did the offence occur?'

'At hotel.'

'There must have been some witnesses, CCTV footage of her leaving,' I say to Locke.

She nods.

I turn my attention back to the screen.

'How old were you?'

'Nineteen.'

'It's a bit of a jump in age, don't you think?'

I can see the questions forming in Locke's head at my remark.

'What happened in the hotel room, Isla?'

'I sit on bed. He take off clothes.'

'His clothes?'

'Yar.'

'And what happened next?'

'I say, don't like. He say, I'm bad man. Big man. I like say no.'

'He liked it when you said no?'

Isla nods.

'He take his tie and on my hands, tie me to bed. He say he like cry. He like hurt.'

'He wanted to make you cry?'

'Yar. He want hurt me.'

'He told you that he wanted to hurt you?'

I turn to Locke who sits shaking her head. 'There's no evidence that he liked it rough.'

'BDSM with prostitutes isn't much different to forcing an underage girl to have sex.'

I glance at the screen to catch Isla bury her head in her hands.

'I say, no. Stop. He . . . no. He like.'

'He liked it?'

'He like pain.'

Isla turns her face away from the camera. I count six seconds before she turns back, her gaze focused on the detective, and see there are no tears in her eyes. No visible distress on her face. Her voice though, says it all. Or is that put on too?

'You said you were happy to go to the papers. Can I ask why you'd want to breach your right to anonymity after the trial, if there is one?'

Isla flushes her fingers.

Money.

'He deserve. He hurt. He pay.'

'Wannabe?' I ask Locke, pausing Isla's face as she stares blankly at the wall.

'Could be. I guess we won't know.'

I offer Locke a curious stare.

'No evidence that he used brothels, hotels, or call girls for that matter. But his daughter . . . seems she's not that innocent herself.'

'What do you mean?'

'They've brought her in. Room five.'

'Same as Wells. She must have really pissed off the Guv. What did she do?'

'Punched a reporter in the face.'

We walk in silence along the corridor.

'Serg,' I say walking past DCI Black, two feet in front of Dawson.

He nods his head in acknowledgement.

'Got another, I see.'

He cocks his head to the side as if not really listening as I jar Locke in the ribs at the sight of the new money plant in the corner of his office. He's always been a sucker for superstitious mumbo-jumbo. I wait until he closes the door of his office behind him before mentioning his lack of speech this morning.

'Trouble at the top?'

'Maybe he's wired wrong.'

The words send a shockwave of an idea to jolt through me.

'Entrapment. Wiring.'

'Yes?' she says, unsure where I'm going with this.

'What if . . .?'

'Spit it out.'

'What reason did Jacky give for the porn links on her phone?'

'She said Antony was using it.'

'She must have known about Sophie then because nothing was deleted.'

'You think she discovered Sophie's conversations with Antony?'

I nod. 'I think we need to pay her a visit. See what she knows.'

'Get her on-side.'

'Prey on his vulnerabilities.'

'Hole in one.'

'When was the last time you played golf?'

'Not since Kez threw my clubs out.'

Locke laughs. I feel like laughing too, but stop dead when Sophie appears in front of me. We skip past one another beyond the entrance. Her face wearing the familiar look of a survivor. Her confidence ripped apart from years of self-hatred and guilt. Ashamed, but determined. Determined not to let her abuser walk free.

'Can I help you?' says Locke, noticing the torn look that sweeps briefly across her addiction-riddled features.

'I . . . I . . . I want to retract my statement. I want to drop the charges.'

KATE

My eyes narrow at the screen through the french windows as the news reporter's face begins to blur.

'The Crown Prosecution Service have decided to charge Mr Antony Wells with two counts of rape. The youngest victim was only seven years old when she claims the vocalist from Blue Wave attacked her.'

I'm glad I didn't go through all those sordid details with the detective. I didn't need to. Antony is going to be vilified by the press. His reputation tarnished. His work destroyed. His freedom stolen.

It's no less than he deserves.

But then DI Locke speaks.

'The original plaintiff has decided not to pursue the allegation.'

I almost drop the phone from my shaking hand.

'But . . . it's on the TV. There's another woman . . .?'

'Her case is different. It won't be tried at the same time.'

'So he might get away with what he did?' *To me.*

'There will be a fair trial.'

'Fair, how is any of this fair?'

'I understand your concern, Kate.' She pauses, then says, 'the CPS can't use your testimony in court. They believe it will damage their case. I'm sorry.'

I can't think past the fact that the woman who

instigated my decision to speak to the police has now left that other woman to face the ordeal of a trial alone.

'Kate, are you still there?'

'Are there more?'

'No other women have come forward.'

I drop the phone onto the grass, feeling bile rise up into my mouth and run from the garden, and into the kitchen. Bent over the sink, I do something I've never done before. I pray.

I pray for this sickness, this black tar inside me to leave.

Empty, drained, and with a sore throat to go with my already thumping headache, I manage to convince myself that Antony Wells is a prolific serial offender and that either thankfully or unfortunately I won't have to stand up in court to face him. But neither will that other woman.

Those sick impulses he has have cost two women their dignity, but including me, his actions have ruined three women's lives. Three women who were so terrified of the consequences, of what the police would say if they spoke out that they kept it inside them all these years. A secret so raw, so painful, that sometimes it hurts to breathe.

Night after night I play over and again the video recording of my past, sending myself to the brink of despair with tearful eyes and dark thoughts. Because of him. Because of people like him.

But although I know it was Antony's actions that sent my life careening off the path it was meant to take, I'm still shrouded in shame, guilt, and self-disgust over my own. Because I didn't act. Because I didn't do anything to stop my abuse. Because I didn't tell anyone.

And if there are more, if I'd have done something, said something, he'd never have been able to hurt another girl. Of that I am certain.

I awake curled up on the floor. My face is wet, and though I know I've been crying, I can't remember doing so. My limbs feel bruised from lying on the hard wood for so long that it takes an age for me to stand.

Steven appears in the doorway.

'Are you alright? What happened? Here, let me help you up,' he says, bending to lift me.

'Are you hurt?'

'No, I . . . tripped. Fell. I'm fine.'

'You don't look fine. Your hair's wet, and . . . have you been crying?'

'Steven, I fell over. Will you just drop it!'

The anger in my words frightens even I, but I don't regret upsetting him. His incessant questions are pissing me off.

'Steven,' I hold out a hand to stop him from moving towards me. I couldn't bear his hands on me right now. 'Steven, please, I fell.'

I laugh, but even *he* seems to notice how false my humour is.

'Okay,' he says.

'I'm going out to get some milk. Do you want anything?'

'I really don't think that's-'

'I'll grab you a beer. What's that one you like called again? Oh, I'll find it, don't worry. I'll see you later.'

I leave the room and head for the stairs.

Steven's eyes follow me as I grab the keys from my handbag and unlock the front door, leaving my purse inside the house.

I can't remember when I started locking myself in the house again. Perhaps it was another automatic reaction to the news about Antony. Or maybe it was before that, after the burglary at number twenty-nine? I don't remember. In fact, I remember very little when I'm under stress. It's just another one of those odd little habits of mine I've grown used to. Like counting the cracks in the pavement as I make my way to the car, and lifting the door handle repeatedly before opening it. Once, twice, three times, for luck.

I drive in no particular direction with the windows up and the air conditioning on so that the cool air blasting in my face both keeps me alert and clouds out the sound of nearby traffic, enabling me to zone out of reality.

Once I've reached the outskirts of Shirehampton, I park on a side street and walk down towards the River Severn and past the football court. It's peaceful here. When the children were small we used to picnic on the grass overlooking the water. I'm reminded of the mother I was then, and crease my face up in disgust. It was awful having to appear normal when all I wanted to do was throw myself into the river and allow the current to pull me away.

At the time I thought all mothers went through that stage. Wanting to run away or end it all to avoid the frustration of living. Keeping your head above the tidal waves of night feeds, sibling rivalry, and forced school holidays is enough to make anyone consider suicide, isn't it?

Don't get me wrong, I love my children. They are my entire world. But, I think that's where the problem stemmed from. I've created two limpets. I need them almost as much as they need me.

I walk towards the boggy tufts of hay that separate the grass field from the water and keep pacing until I find myself on the slippery verge. There is only a four-foot drop to the Avon river below. I dangle one of my plimsole covered feet over the muddied water and pull it away the moment I hear a child wail from somewhere nearby. I glance back to see a toddler hurtling through the tall grass away from her mother, towards the river.

'Darling?' the woman cries.

I move swiftly towards the little girl who stands several feet away, sizing me up for a few moments before holding out her hand for me to take.

'You mustn't trust strangers so easily,' I tell her, taking her hand and walking her back to her distraught honey-haired mother.

'She just ran off,' she says exasperated.

'It's good luck that I was here.'

You should be taking better care of her.

'Thank you,' she says, pulling her daughter close and walking back to where she's parked the buggy.

The two-and-a-half-year-old girl seemed to understand that in that moment I needed her. If she hadn't come down to the waters edge I don't know what I would have done.

TERESA

There was a knock on the door. I was wearing a dressing gown, about to slip out the back door for a cigarette. Until a year ago I hadn't smoked since trying it at the age of fourteen with some friends on our way to school. Gillian had stolen some cigarettes from her father, who hadn't noticed. The pull of it was too much for me. I needed something, anything to cope with the daily discontent that Antony created in our small little lives.

I'd been awake since 5:30am when the sun began to creep up from the horizon. And, as I lay there, the nocturnal sounds slowly being replaced by bird song and the familiar rocking movement coming from behind the other side of my bedroom wall, I was once again alerted to Antony's morning routine of bouncing on his bed, until I opened the door and told him to stop.

I sent him down for breakfast and made my way downstairs some time later to find the kitchen empty. He'd gone out for one of his excursions again. Where he went, I'd no idea but his walks often took him down to the cemetery. On a still morning, I often found him sat on a bench humming to himself in Canford park, or more recently in the gardens of the crematorium. The place sent little chills of ice down my spine at the memory of burying my mother, and then my father. Antony enjoyed the peace and quiet such a place offered him. That morning though, he hadn't been for his usual walk.

I opened the door to find two policemen stood in front of me, their faces grim. I knew it could only mean Antony had caused trouble for someone again, and a wave of nausea washed over me as I lead them inside. They both seated themselves opposite me and took far too long to get to the point of their visit.

'The woman doesn't want to press charges, but we have an obligation to record the incident.'

'But, he's just a child.'

'Ms Carter, we're very sorry, but garden theft is a criminal offence and-'

'He won't do it again. He's just a boy. He has . . .' I didn't know how to word it. 'Problems.'

They both looked at each other then. Two men who didn't know my son, thinking they had the authority to tell me what was best for him.

'If that stays on his record-'

'It's not a formal report. Just a note. We have to report any incidents we're affronted with during our shift. It's nothing personal Ms-'

'Just call me Teresa. And, I understand. Please be assured that nothing like this has ever happened before and it won't happen again. I'll be having words with Antony, don't you worry.'

I had no idea if they believed me or not, but I hoped it would be the end of the matter. Antony had stolen sweets from the newsagents before and he'd had a few fights in school, but never anything of this magnitude. Sneaking around someone's house in the early hours of the morning. I couldn't understand what he got from such an odd activity. It didn't make any sense. I had no idea why the woman had alerted the police. Surely she could see that he was young, a bit dim? I should have grown used to the senselessness of Antony's behaviour long before then because nothing he did seemed normal to me, but even that surprised me.

What the hell was he doing?

Once the officers had left, I waited for Antony to climb down off the wall in the front garden and come inside before I mentioned anything. For once, his head was bowed. He must have known what he'd done was wrong. When he looked up at me with glassy eyes and apologised for the first time in his life, I was stunned.

I lay my hand on his shoulder and lead him inside. Taking a seat at the small dining table I asked him why he'd done it.

'I wanted to see her.'

I had to force myself to stay calm.

'You wanted to see who?'

'The girl.'

'You know it's not right, what you did, don't you?'

'I just wanted to watch her sleeping.'

I stayed with him, trying to impress upon him the reason why it was so wrong to sneak up to someone's window and stare at them through the glass, but he didn't seem to understand. I cut our discussion short when I realised the time.

'We have to get you to school. Go and get your uniform on.'

He went upstairs to dress while I fumbled around the kitchen, preparing a packed lunch of Spam sandwiches, an apple, and a yoghurt. All the while, trying to keep the buzzing in my head at bay. Antony wasn't like other boys. He wasn't like anyone I'd ever known. I decided that whatever was wrong with him must be a unique problem and that it was going to take some convincing his teachers and our doctor, to find out what it was. But I vowed that I would.

That morning, after dropping Antony off to school I headed into work and went over my tea break and lunch so that my boss would be more inclined to allow me to leave an hour early. By the time I made it to the library I only had half an hour left before I had to walk back down the hill to collect Antony from school.

I flicked through shelves of texts relating to abnormal psychology, childhood diseases and education before I found what I was looking for. It was a thick tome, containing referenced material from various sources regarding child development. I took it straight to the desk to where the woman sat. She stamped the book, giving me a fortnight to return it and I left, hurrying quickly towards the school.

Later that evening, after running Antony a bath, I gave him a hefty supper I hoped would keep him nailed to his bed long enough for me to take a quick glance through the textbook, and began leafing through the pages. When I came across a section on childhood disorders written by a very well educated doctor in the field of paediatric medicine, I thought I'd found what I'd been looking for.

In 1965, Dr Erik Erikson had written a scholarly article about childhood developmental disorders which was published in a journal and quoted within the text of the book I was reading. I remember almost exactly what it said because I was astonished at its accuracy regarding Antony's symptoms. Developmental disorders in children involved, amongst other things, language delay, low intelligence, fecal incontinence and a lack of appropriate social skills and behaviour. A few pages in there was mention of a Dr John Bowlby and Dr Donald Winnicott who together expressed that aggression was a healthy aspect of a childs development. I read with earnest, trying to picture how these specialists came to such contrasting conclusions when I happened to come across a theory by Dr Melanie Klein, who suggested that age regression and poor motor skills were signs of bonding problems between the child and his or her caregiver. In other words, my parenting skills weren't up to scratch and I'd spawned a child with an anxious-avoidant attachment to his mother.

According to everything I read, there was an array of learning difficulties associated with children, like Antony, who exhibited the types of problems I had to contend with. One of which was autism. But even that potential diagnosis didn't seem to fit. For one, it didn't explain Antony's constant crying, which according to Bowlby and Winnicott meant that he was normal or according to Klein meant that he was not receiving the care he needed from me. Neither did the book explain why Antony grew angry quickly for no reason over the most minuscule things, or why his outbursts often included violence. Although later on in the book there was mention of Attention Deficit Hyperactivity Disorder which included a lack of impulse control, but that didn't sound like Antony. He was more inclined to remain seated for long periods of time, completing the same task repeatedly over and again. He also didn't fare well with change. By the time I'd finished reading the book I was still just as clueless as to what was wrong with him as I had been before I'd opened the damn thing.

Antony was sometimes a calm, quiet child. He loved animals. He invited a stray cat into our home once, just after our holiday to Woolacombe Bay. We'd found Spot wandering up and down the back garden from the gate to the potting shed until Antony placed a bowl of tuna down onto the path and it crept up and ate it, demanding more the moment it was gone. The cat lived in Antony's room and seemed to be as involved in singular activity as he. Once, when I opened his bedroom door both Spot and Antony were self-absorbed in their own activities. Neither of them glanced at me as I switched the light off for them to sleep. Which is why I couldn't understand how, despite many of the symptoms of autism I'd read about, it didn't say how caring autistic-minded children were towards others, especially animals. I was not the mother those texts painted me to be. I did not refuse to physically comfort my son, he didn't ask for it. I was not emotionally unresponsive to his needs, he didn't require stimulation. He was happy in his own little world, wasn't he?

I discovered why Antony had killed the bird that had flown too close to him. He hadn't meant to. Just as he hadn't meant to kill the goldfish he thought would prefer living in the bath. He'd forgotten to leave the plug in when he'd left the bathroom because the action was habitual. He'd watched it helplessly sliding down the drain, unsure of what to do to save him. He liked to take care of animals. He was always good with younger

114

children too. He had an affinity with smaller beings, anyone more vulnerable than he. But his attitude towards adults was ambivalent. Baffling. When I did manage to coax him to look into my eyes he did so with indifference, hostility even.

Still, I've no idea what makes a child detest winged beings: birds, but have a love of fish, cats, dogs, and small children. I don't know why Antony displayed many of the signs of autism, but not explicitly. Is it some form of a continuum? A set of scales? I thought.

Of course, I didn't know back then that autistic spectrum disorder was in fact, a multilayered, multifaceted set of problems that appeared as uniquely individual as the children that suffered from them. Despite knowing this now, even clinical psychologists, consultant paediatricians, and doctors have no idea what causes it. The signs were there back then. But they didn't increase in severity until Antony's father walked back into our lives.

Once Christopher decided he did, after all, want something to do with his son, Antony had already reached the difficult age of ten. And from there, his life went downhill- fast.

DI SILVER

Today, the small house that felt homely when we'd come to charge Antony, looks uncared for, feels cramped. I get the impression that Antony gave it the light the building is now lacking, but can't reason why.

'Well, I ain't got all day,' says Jacky through brown teeth, offering me a seat beside her on the shabby sofa.

'I'll get to the point, Mrs Wells,' says Locke. 'The phone you reported Antony used, your phone, we found a lot of incriminating evidence on it.'

'What's that got to do with me?'

Diving straight to her defence, I sense something amiss.

'We've had a graphologist take a look at the words used when Antony was in discussions with Sophie-'

'He spoke to the girl?'

'He did. Our expert thinks it's likely that you knew about those conversations.'

'I didn't know nothing,' she says, sharply.

Didn't, not don't?

I decide a more friendly approach might be useful in weaving a way through her hostility.

'How was your sex life, Mrs Wells?'

'Good. Better than good.'

'Could you explain what you mean by that?'

'I like it a lot, no harm in that.'

'Did you ever feel uncomfortable with anything your husband did?'

'No.'

'Were there ever any affairs?'

'My husband is a loyal man, detective.'

The strained atmosphere begins to make even Locke appear uncomfortable. I notice her shudder, but not from the cool wind blowing in through the open bay windows, rather from Jacky's gait. She doesn't appear comfortable, settled. Then I realise why. The room is untidy not from a lack of cleaning, but from packing. There are several suitcases stuffed on top of one another behind the door.

'Are you going somewhere, Mrs Wells?'

'To my sister's. Can't stay 'ere while all this is goin' on.'

'Could you give us an address, just in case we need to get in touch with you again?'

She takes her time to leave the sofa, struggling to shift her weight, returning to hand me a slip of paper with an address scrawled on it.

'Couldn't find a pen,' she says, by way of explaining the action taking her several minutes to perform.

'Thank you for your time.'

'Yeah, well, you gotta do your job ain't you.'

I follow Locke to the door and feel my shoulders relax as we step outside.

'The atmosphere in that house is tense,' says Locke.

'She's hiding something.'

'You think she knew about Sophie?'

'I think she knows a lot about something, but I don't know if it's got anything to do with Sophie. You think she knows about his problem?'

'It's a problem now is it?'

'A sexual offence is an extreme form of addiction, don't you think?'

'I don't think it has anything to do with impulse control.'

'Then what makes a man commit such a heinous crime?'

'You're the new expert on criminal profiling, what do you think?'

I baulk at her candid response.

'It's a basic psychology course,' I repeat for the third time this week. 'I'm no expert on psychopathology, but I know a liar when I see one.'

'What kind of woman would stay with a man who does that to innocent young girls?'

'And women.'

'Oh, yeah, well, Isla's case is apparently too difficult for us to deal with so the Met are taking care of her.'

'I hope they are.'

'You don't believe her?' Locke looks shocked.

'It's my job to believe *all* victims.'

Locke shakes her head. 'Don't.'

'What?'

'Don't say what you're thinking. You'll regret it.'

I'll keep my doubt to myself then.

'How's the report coming along?'

'I'll call the Guv, see if Dr Cotes has finalised his assessment on Antony's mental health.'

'I suppose it won't hurt,' she says, pressing the key into the ignition and hitting the accelerator a little more forcefully than usual.

KATE

I enjoyed my little jaunt yesterday. It seems to have recharged my batteries. I used to do a lot of power walking when I was stressed out. When the children were small I used to push Daryl in a buggy whilst Lisa hung onto one handle for dear life. As they got older I used to drive out of Bristol and park up somewhere secluded. Even with a toddler in hand, another in the buggy, we walked for miles. My legs still ache, I haven't had a trek in so long, but the freedom I felt whilst ambling away from my dull ordered life, to find myself stood in the centre of a field with no recollection of how I'd got there frees my spirit. I feel as though I could soar through the clouds, soak up the sun. The life force. The energy.

Escape.

Today DI Locke wears a navy blue V-neck shirt with black slacks. I wonder how she can wear such dark colours in this heat, but she doesn't seem to mind. Her deep chestnut eyes and open posture immediately make me warm to her just as I'd done as I gave her the gap-filled inventory of those two years where I spent most of my time. The facts were fictionalised, not to protect Antony, but to protect my own secret.

Breaking the silence on something that has been lying dormant in the back of my mind for so long it's almost become another part of me, should have been a major step in my healing journey. A journey broken by rough rides through hilly terrains and slouching puddles of murky water. But, all I've done is create a break. A stop-gap.

I've been living with my secret for over half of my life. Two decades ago, at the age of twenty-four, I attended counselling in a converted house a short bus ride from the flat I'd started renting. I hadn't met Steven yet, but I vowed I'd begin with a clean slate as soon as we started dating. I made a silent promise not to speak of the past, and I haven't. For years I've battled my way through life struggling to survive, until a few years ago when I realised I'd begun to thrive. Post-Traumatic growth it's called. The counsellor I met with in the early days called me brave, resilient and strong, and until two weeks ago, I'd begun to accept those terms.

But now all I see are lies.

When I answered the phone yesterday I felt my world collapsing all around me, but somehow just knowing those two other women are going through the same torment as I makes me feel less alone. I'm not glad that monster got his claws into those girls, but knowing the horrific abuse they've suffered hasn't made them any more specially indifferent than I - as I'd been taught to believe - makes it easier to bear the scars I've accumulated since Antony entered my life. And believe me, there are many. I keep them covered with long-sleeved shirts, or like today, with hundreds of thick beaded bracelets, but the faint lines across my wrists and thighs are visible if you look close enough.

I didn't have to come in, but I'm not due back to work

until Monday, and Steven will begin to suspect that I've been fired if he returns home to find me back before him so I've decided to come down to the station to speak to DI Locke. It seems to me that she does far more paperwork and behind the scenes investigating than interviewing suspects and witnesses. I'm a witness, according to her not a victim. Unbeknown to her though, I'm a survivor.

She turns her grey swivel chair towards me and says, 'Kate, I wasn't expecting you.'

She doesn't seem offended by my interruption but does appear confused. Unsure of my reason for being here.

'I need to know more about the woman he's . . .'

'Follow me,' she says, standing up from behind her desk and leading me down a wide corridor and into a small room. She waits for me to take a seat before replying to my earlier question.

'I can't give you any more information than I already have. It's confidential, you know that.'

I do know that.

'Are there others?'

'What makes you think that there might be other women who haven't yet come forward?'

I leave the station and make my way back to the car, parked on the corner just down from the new grotesquely modern grey Bristol Royal Infirmary building. The street for this time of day is as crowded as ever due to the upcoming Harbour Festival this weekend. Street sellers and visitors from around the country are packing up to spend a few nights here. And along with the daily commuters and local office workers, I feel hemmed in as I weave my way through the traffic away from the city centre towards home. I travel through St. Pauls and the length of Ashley Road with the smell of cannabis and delicious Carribean foods emanating from nearby shops, flooding the car and my nostrils. I drive up the hill and along past the Brunel college before remembering I told Steven I'd buy food for dinner tonight.

I stop off in the Co-Op on the corner for some wholegrain rice and herb coated salmon, hoping it will be enough to fulfil Steven's healthy appetite. I'll have to eat as well so I don't appear to be suffering from anorexia at the dining table, despite rarely feeling hungry.

Steven is approaching the house as I reverse into a parking space.

He greets me at the door, appearing surprised.

'You had time to go shopping?'

'I got an hour off as one of my clients has C-Diff. They don't want any of us to go in.'

'That's contagious, isn't it?'

'Yes, but I'm all up to date on my vaccinations and-'

'What did you buy?' he says, rooting through the carrier bag I hold in one hand as I slam the car door shut and lock it with the other.

'Fish.'

He pulls a face, and smiles.

'I'll bite you, you ungrateful sod.'

'Don't make promises you can't keep.'

I know what he's getting at. We haven't had sex in

over a week. It's unlike me. But I intend to prove to him that I'm still madly in love with him tonight. Even if I have to fake arousal.

I don't enjoy lying to my husband, it's just become a recent necessary evil. One which I have to indulge in a little bit longer if I am to continue the pretence that everything between us hasn't changed and that my past isn't going to affect us, despite knowing the complete opposite is true. I don't want him to think there's anything wrong with me or that I've become distant from him. But I'm certainly not going to tell him about Antony Wells until a court date has been made, and maybe not even then. I want to see him sent to prison before I tell Steven anything.

I'm aware that I'm deliberately stalling things, and I know that once the date has been set, the truth will have to come out. I'm just hoping it won't be too soon. I'm still trying to get my head around his arrest, his charge. I never thought he deserved to live, but now the chance to secure justice for what happened to me is a real possibility, I'm looking forward to seeing him suffer.

I wonder what prisoners do to men like him?

I slug off my work plimsolls (I had to give the impression of going to work even if my only intention was to skive off) and make my way into the kitchen to undress. Shoving my clothes inside the machine and turning them onto a boil wash, unnecessary, but worthwhile if I'm to convince Steven of my whereabouts today. I saunter down the hall towards the stairs where Steven meets me with a wink before pulling me towards him to wrap his arms around my naked waist.

'I've missed this,' he says, kissing me hard on my

neck and face.

'It's only been a week.'

He moves away from me, looking sadly into my eyes.

'What?' I say, jokingly.

'We haven't had sex in months, Kate.'

Has it really been that long?

The truth is, I can't remember.

TERESA

I stood at the door, shocked and a little pissed off that despite not having wanted anything to do with Antony for years, Christopher had decided that now would be a good time to show up out of the blue. I'd kept in contact with his mother, sending her the occasional Christmas card and the like so assumed she must have been the one to give him our new address. I didn't have many friends, and the ones I did have were a select few of women from the school. Nobody else knew where we lived.

'What do you want?'

I didn't mean to be so forthright, but under the circumstances, I found it ludicrous that he thought waltzing into our lives the moment he felt like it was okay. And, he seemed to want to pick up with Antony where he left off, despite his son not knowing him from the milk man.

'I came to see my boy.'

'Well, he's not a boy anymore. And he's in school until 3:30pm.'

'I'll come with you to pick him up.'

'I don't think that's a very good idea.'

'I have rights, you know. I want to see my son.'

'Well now isn't a convenient time because-'

'I'll wait here.'

'I was about to make some lunch.'

'Why are you making this difficult Teresa?'

'You can't just show up and demand to see him.'

'I know this is difficult for you, but can't we put aside our differences? I just want to see little Antony.'

'Fine, come in. But, I warn you, he's not so little these days.'

'Been feeding him up I see,' he said, pointing to a photograph on the mantlepiece as he followed me inside the living room.

Was he trying to imply Antony was fat?

'Sit down. I'll be back in a moment.'

I took my time to butter the bread, slice some ham, and cut the sandwich in half. I boiled the kettle and ate whilst making myself a cup of tea. By the time I returned to the living room Christopher was fidgeting on the armchair by the window, glancing at his watch then at the shelving unit behind him where I kept some photographs of Antony when he was younger.

'Turned into a fine strapping lad hasn't he, Tee?'

I ignored the nickname he'd given me when we were together. I didn't want him to know how annoyed I was at his comment regarding Antony's weight, so I bit my lip. It wasn't my fault all he did these days was eat and sit in front of his games console. I tried to get Antony to go out and play with his friends, but I'd recently discovered that the lads he liked to hang around with, who lived only a few streets away were much older than him. Steering him away from them meant he rarely left the house after school.

As the clock approached 3:00pm I decided to leave early, hoping the long walk to the school to collect Antony would wear Christopher down. I thought the brisk exercise would send him home quicker. I was wrong. We ended up taking Antony to the park.

When Christopher approached him, I had to gently explain to him who Christopher was and why he was there. Antony didn't usually deal well with change and would often hurl items at me in frustration when things weren't going his way or when his regular routine had been broken. Like the recent dental appointment which resulted in him biting me.

But this time, Antony didn't appear bothered by his father's sudden re-entrance into his life so I gladly went along with the idea of a trip to the playing fields. I sat beside Christopher in silence. A scream forced me to turn around and I leapt off the bench when I saw the body of a small boy, no older than six, lying in a heap on the concrete beneath the slide, sobbing uncontrollably, blood spurting from a gash on his forehead.

I knew despite Christopher's protestations that Antony was somehow involved in the incident, and that it hadn't been an accident at all, but Christopher looked at me as though I'd been talking about someone else's child.

'No son of mine would do a wicked thing like that.'

The trouble was, that was exactly the sort of thing Antony would do, he just didn't realise it yet.

Once we got home I sat Antony down to explain to us what had happened. Christopher shot me a look of disgust at even considering his son capable of such a vicious, unprovoked act of violence, but I looked into Antony's eyes and knew what he was going to say even before he spoke.

'He said I was stupid.'

'So you pushed him?'

'I didn't mean to. My hand slipped out.'

Christopher stuttered and said that perhaps the boy had been asking for it by upsetting him. I waited until Antony had retreated upstairs to play on his games console before closing the living room door for a bit of privacy. I had no idea that Antony had crept downstairs to fetch a glass of milk and some biscuits from the kitchen. He heard every word I said.

'You have no fucking idea, do you?'

'Tee?'

I held out my hand and stopped him from having a go at me for swearing.

'Antony isn't like other children. There've been many more incidents like this that I can't even count. He's not normal. He has issues, and-'

'Tee, there's nothing wrong with my son. Maybe if you'd have-'

'Don't you dare,' I cut in. 'Don't you dare criticise my parenting skills. You haven't been around. Perhaps he wouldn't be the way he is if he'd had a father.'

'So you're not with anybody?'

'I barely have enough time to go to work. Don't look at me like that. What else was I supposed to do, claim benefits? I have to keep a roof over our heads and food on the table, seeing as you . . .'

What's the point, he doesn't care.

'Tee, I want to help you. Give you money-'

'It's too late for that now.'

'You can't deny me the right to financially support my child.'

'Money isn't going to solve this, and he's no longer a

child. He's in junior school. He has many of the things we never had as children. We're doing alright on my measly salary and your monthly *allowance*, thank you.'

He stood up then. 'Maybc I haven't done enough, but I'm going to help you to take care of him. Maybe there's something we can do, someone he can see.'

'You mean a doctor?'

'There has to be a reason why he's so angry and out of control.'

'Oh, you haven't seen the half of it yet.'

I proceeded to enlighten Christopher of all the things that had happened over the years. I told him that I'd read up on it and that I was still none the wiser as to what was actually wrong with him.

'That's why we should take him to see a doctor. They'll know what it is and how to treat it.'

How naive he was back then, believing that all we had to do was show a united front and take Antony to see a specialist, secure a diagnosis, and apply the prescribed treatment. But these things don't work out like that. It would take us many years to discover what was wrong with Antony, and by then it would be too late. The damage had been done.

DI SILVER

'The prison smells, I'll never get used to them.'

'The smell of repentance?'

'No, mashed potato and weak gravy.'

Dr Cotes is a thin man of average height, and as usual appears impeccably dressed. I usually meet him in the office, but today he is exceptionally busy assessing a couple who killed their son in a fire in order to claim on the insurance so I'm meeting him between appointments.

'Take a seat, please,' he says. 'I'm sorry, I don't have long. I'm meeting with my client in fifteen minutes.'

'The mother?'

'The father, actually. The mother has been referred to a psychiatric unit for further assessment.'

You must have an unstable personality to kill your own child for a few measly thousand, I think, perching myself beside Dr Cotes.

The room is tight and the lack of sunlight makes it hard to breathe inside the small box-like room.

'It's the broom cupboard,' he says, offering no further explanation. But I assume the room he is forced to use comes from great pressure to the UK prison service from a government who dislike ploughing money *into* anything.

They're short-staffed and under-resourced.

'How can I help you, detective?'

I was hoping to catch Dr Cotes before he files his clinical report to the CPS.

'I was wondering how your assessment on Mr Wells was coming along?'

'You mean is my client suffering from an incapacitated understanding of his arrestable offence? You shall be disappointed. However, he has disclosed some interesting things which I am not inclined to discuss with you.'

'He's of sound mind?'

'As sound as they come. He has, what is termed a split diagnoses, but nothing atypical in cases involving a sexual offence towards a child.'

'What is your diagnosis?'

'I can't disclose anything that isn't relevant to the court or which might otherwise be unknown.'

His use of fancy words and inability to answer the question directly is starting to irritate me.

He leans forward in his chair, 'you want to know is he mad or bad?'

'In a nutshell.'

Locke folds her arms in front of her, a posture to mean she's as impatient as I.

'I don't think he's either.'

'Dangerous then?'

'Antony's is a complex puzzle of a case. For one, he has no obvious lack of emotional regulation or congnitive impairment one might find in psychopathic or sociopathic personality, for instance. However, he shares some charactristics with individuals who display autistic spectrum disorder or asperger's syndrome. Secondly, although, he does seem to lack IQ function, it's at a relatively low level, and not necessarily the cause of his obvious difficulty with social skills. But thirdly, and more importantly, there were without a doubt some difficulties expressed in the re-telling of his childhood. A strained relationship with mother, who seemed at times emotionally inhibited. And, according to Antony, his father left when he was very young, reappearing when he was around age ten which added more strain onto his relationship with his mother.'

'A common theme in sexual offenders.'

'Mmm.'

'Quite a puzzle then?' says Locke, feigning interest.

'I've concluded that Mr Wells shows a moderate level of autism accompanied by a difficult, challenging view of the world, potentially resulting from an upbringing which involved an emotionally neglectful mother who often didn't speak to him for days on end, coupled by a criminal background in his youth. All of these things together do not cause an individual to sexually offend, as you know Paul, but it might help the trial if everyone involved show a little empathy towards my client's mental health needs.'

'How does this affect the case?' says Locke.

'I will ensure that Antony receives the support he needs throughout the trial and afterwards, if required.'

I assume he means some kind of offending treatment programme.

'I've read that they're only ten percent effective.'

'If delivered at the appropriate time. Of course we have no idea how many years Antony has been offending for. He's still pleading not guilty.'

KATE

I haul myself out of bed, delirious and foggy headed. I hardly slept at all last night. After we'd had sex, I felt so tired I collapsed in Steven's arms and lay there in the darkness listening to him snore. The sounds of the night replacing the whirring in my head. The distant hum of traffic from the main road and a few hours later birdsong. I make my way downstairs, sleep-deprived and irritable.

After glugging down a strong cup of coffee I make my way back upstairs to dress when the phone rings in the hallway. I press the phone to my ear just before it rings out.

'Kate, I'm glad I've caught you. Have you got a minute?'

Shit. It's Ruth from work.

'Sure,' I yawn.

'It's just that . . . is everything alright? You haven't been well recently and we've had a case of norovirus going around. It's hitting everyone really hard this one, and I just thought, well . . .'

'Ruth. I'm fine.'

'The boss has been asking after you.'

I knew this was coming. I've never spent more than a day off work with a stomach bug, and it's crawling into a week now.

'Ruth, I'm fine. Really.'

To tell you the truth, I've been feeling really tired and I'm having trouble sleeping. In fact, I think I'm having some kind of breakdown.

'Will you be able to make it in on Monday?'

'Without a doubt.'

'It's just that we're very short-staffed at the moment. You know how it is.'

'I'll be there.'

'Great. I'll see you then.'

We exchange a quick goodbye before I hang up.

I should have expected a call from my supervisor. She's the company gossip, but a very caring colleague. I can't afford to lose my job, along with everything else. I can't let Antony spoil things for me. He's ruined enough of my years already, to take my career too would be the final straw.

I leave the living room and decide that as the sun is peeking out from behind the clouds I should take the opportunity to enjoy it before the inevitable rain closes in. It's late Summer now and I decide to take advantage of it. I must admit, despite having fallen into a comfortable trap of keeping my mind busy with work and household chores, I have enjoyed taking some time out to relax. It's good for the soul, as Steven would say.

I leave the house, deciding to take a walk around the park. I take a detour to the library on the way. I haven't been inside one since the children were small. The familiar smell of musty paper and the quiet, calm atmosphere soothes the constant impulse to scream. I leave with a paperback copy of a best-selling title by one of my favorite authors and sit under a tree in one corner of Canford Park, watching a family picnicking. A young boy kicks a ball into the trees and a dog comes up to me, sniffing for food, only to turn around and saunter off when he realises I have nothing more interesting than some bound paper in my hand.

When the children were small we'd spend a lot of time in the park. My eyes glaze over at the memory of birds chirping above our heads as we wandered through the trees with the sun on our backs. But I don't think I'm remembering it right because even then there was this shadow cast over everything. A darkness that threatened to penetrate all I held dear. I always wondered if it was within me. I was never able to fully surrender to the present and enjoy soaking in my surroundings.

As I sit here, people watching, I notice a family of five playing football, laughing; a mother following her toddler along the path towards the pond. But, even now, I wonder if the smile the little boy acting as goalkeeper wears is fake. What secrets does the lone girl treading carefully into the undergrowth hide behind those deep wide eyes? To others she might appear to be searching for fairies, but I'm wondering what troubles may lurk beneath her introverted gait.

I still look at everyone, trying to decide whether they fall into the typology of a potential abuser or victim. To be able to see the world only as though through a black and white lense is an affliction I've carried for years. Even medication aimed at suppressing the anxiety merely blurs the edges, softens the sharp colours of reality. But if I lift the veil a little I can still see the blemishes in others, the shades of grey, the hidden gaps between sentences, notice the space between people.

Harsh, I know, to look at the world this way, but distrust is a powerful precursor to denial.

I find myself stood at the entrance to the park staring at nothing. I don't notice the book I've left on the grass, its pages flapping in the breeze. All I feel is the heavy ache, a yearning so deep and pure I cannot fight the urge to run. But as I do, I know, I'm running from myself, my conscience.

My heart begins to thud against my chest. My ribs tighten as I gasp for breath. My feet slap the pavement as I dart between people, unsure which direction I'm aiming for. I have to get away from this place. There are too many people. People with secrets, disguising their true intentions behind kind metaphor. All full of shit.

I want to go home. I need to feel the safety of those four walls pinning me into the bubble of security I've created, stopping me from doing something stupid.

TERESA

At the age of fifteen Antony decided he'd outgrown his games console and spent much of his spare time in the park with his friends, Nathan and Dominic. Both boys were seventeen and I'd given up trying to coax Antony into making friends with some boys his own age. He spent a lot of time with one of our neighbour's little girls until they'd moved away. I never understood why most of Antony's friends were either still in primary school or years older. I had to admit though, he seemed to have matured in the few short months Nathan and Dominic had befriended him.

The two boys were childhood friends, growing up together on the council estate in Southmead. Both of them were streetwise and looked as though they'd had a hard life. It was good that Antony had the time for them because it seemed nobody else did.

Until Nathan was arrested for dealing cannabis, I had no idea what the little sods were getting up to. I suppose you could say I turned a blind eye to their petty criminal activities until it affected Antony. He was with Dominic when he'd stolen a car. He'd driven it around the estate for almost two hours before a policeman stopped him. He didn't give in to the thrill of a chase as I later heard Dominic had wanted to. Antony left the car with his head down, pretending to cry for his mum. Dominic was placed into Feltham Young Offenders institute, and Antony, bless him, didn't have the heart to tell the arresting officer they'd both been driving the vehicle. He waited until he was released from his interview before confiding in me.

'It was Dom's idea, mum. It's just that Dom was driving when we were caught.'

'I can't believe you'd be so irresponsible. What if you'd hit someone? You might have seriously injured somebody or heaven forbid, killed them. Without a licence, insurance . . . Doesn't the idea of spending years in prison terrify you?'

I knew it was a stupid thing to say the moment the words left my mouth because Antony lacked the ability to forward think. He was impulsive by nature and he didn't understand social etiquette. He never set out to do dangerous, illegal things, but it was obvious that he couldn't comprehend *why* they were dangerous or illegal.

My mind would often drift back to the early days of his life where I'd try to pinpoint where exactly it had all gone wrong. What had I done to deserve a son who didn't think twice about punching someone in the face if he thought they'd looked at him the wrong way? Where did his sudden loss of control, the terrifying rage come from?

I had no idea what those early warning signs were telling me back then, but I do now.

I read somewhere recently that impulsivity, truancy, getting into trouble with the police from a young age and cognitive impairment were classic signals for future offending behaviour. I don't remember who wrote it or where I read it but it makes sense, I suppose.

I always knew Antony was going to end up in prison, but never for something like rape.

DI SILVER

The investigation has stalled somewhat. There are no new leads and the entire office is quietly concentrating on their next case. A man accused of horrific sex attacks on women in the Fishponds area. He uses a knife to lure his victims into the tree-lined space at the back of Eastville Park before raping them.

Locke appears at my side, winding a piece of hair around her finger, an obvious gesture that the cogs are turning in her head.

'What's on your mind?'

'Isla is reluctant to speak at the trial.'

'Even under VIPER link?'

'As soon as the Met mentioned the trial, she closed up.'

'Talking of Wells, I've been thinking . . .'

'You have a theory?'

'Antony's speech cues clearly mark him out as having a lack of social comprehension, learning difficulties, etc. so how did he manage to hold a conversation with Sophie for hours at a time?'

'I'm not following you.'

'The dialogue found on Jacky's phone between Antony Wells and Sophie Anderson indicates a slight difference between the way he speaks and the way he writes.'

'I thought that. But didn't Tara pick up on this?'

'She said the difference was minute.'

'You think someone else was talking to Sophie?'

'It's a possibility.'

'The mother, Jacky, is an obvious choice.'

'You got the impression she knew something when we spoke to her.'

'Yes, but we can't assume she was aware that her husband was abusing girls.'

'She left Bristol pretty quick after his arrest.'

'Okay, where's that address she gave us?'

KATE

I've spent the last few days feeling wretched. It's the same way I used to feel when the depression had come to envelope me in its cloak of darkness. There doesn't seem to be any reason to get up in the morning, and if it weren't for the fact that I'd agreed to return to work, I would have stayed in bed.

Steven is beginning to suspect that there is something seriously wrong with our marriage. Last night he asked me if I was keeping something from him. He spoke about trust and loyalty. Although he hasn't accused me of anything, I get the impression he assumes I'm having an affair. Which, after everything I've been through is ridiculous, but of course, he doesn't know anything about my past. I understand he's confused, worried even, but the truth is, I can't bear another man looking at me. The thought of anyone but Steven touching me makes my skin crawl.

Apart from Steven, my only sexual experiences are the ones that occurred in that house thirty years ago. The memory propels me out of bed, clutching my nightdress for support. I clamber down the stairs, dressing in front of the spin dryer, unable to bear the sight of our bed as I tug the uniform over my head and brush it down, checking for creases.

The only other time I've felt like this - complete and

utter helplessness in the years intervening now and *then* - was when I was in labour with the children. Being forced to lie flat on my back, legs apart, helpless, vulnerable, and my body in agony was almost too much to bear. A jolt of pain shoots down my stomach as flashes of memory beat across my eyes like a tattoo.

I manage to force down a slice of toast, swallowing it back with a cup of strong coffee, heading for the door to start the morning shift by 7:00am.

It's cold and the sky is a mottled patchwork of slate grey, black and thick white clouds that threaten to burst with heavy rain at any moment. I count the cracks in the pavement- fourteen now the roots of the fern trees dotting the concrete are forcing the ground upwards. Trees are strong, unlike me I think, closing the door behind me and clenching the steering wheel tightly, before I release and reapply the handbrake three times. A new compulsion I hadn't noticed I'd begun until today.

Sometimes I wonder when these odd ideas first took hold, but self-analysis rarely provides an answer I'm happy with. So long as it doesn't bother anyone else, my actions aren't a problem. The one and only time Steven noticed me lock the front door, open it, lock it again and repeat the performance until I was satisfied nobody could break in he accepted my excuse and never mentioned it again. I said I'd caught my coat in the door.

There have been other times since but I've always managed to excuse my actions with trapped fingers, a caught jumper or having forgotten something from the car. Only recently has he begun to take an interest in my moods, looking at me as though testing my sanity against his own. I suppose knowing he takes me, flaws and all enables me to keep up the charade of being normal. I don't remember when the counting began, but it's been a habit for a very long time.

The time lapses began as I teenager. At first, I'd walk into a room and simply forget why I was there, or find myself stood in the centre of a staircase, unsure if I was going up or coming down. Then, years later, there were times when I convinced myself I'd lost one of the children and became hysterical. Running frantically through the house searching behind the sofa, in cupboards, screaming their names as I stood at the bottom of the garden that faced onto the back of the neighbouring houses, enraged when I found them asleep or playing quietly in their bedroom, looking up at me from the floor with huge curious eyes, wondering what was wrong with me.

These days, missing hours have become the norm. Since the first suicide attempt, they occur less frequently. I excused having taken too many sleeping pills as an accident. A momentary lapse of concentration. Steven assumed I'd fallen asleep, but when he struggled to wake me, finding the empty bottle under the pillow, he'd called an ambulance. Forced to acknowledge how close I'd come to losing not only my life but my family in such a sudden, brutal way gave me the impetus to move forwards. At least I thought it had, until recent events which have left me unsure if I ever will.

If I was no longer here, who would protect my grandchildren from potential abusers? Of course, Steven would do his best, just as my father had, but that never saved me, did it?

I make it into work just before the first fat droplets of rain begin to fall down hard from a dark purple sky. The same shade Ms Smythes wears over her eye. The bruise a visible reminder of her fall last week. Guilt, something I'm used to now, comes in waves, threatening to tarnish what little time we have together. The carer who came to her aid wasn't me, the woman she's used to, and it pains me to see the distress such a small accident has marked on her.

She twitches in her chair, hands clenched tight in her lap when she hears the letterbox opening, two envelopes falling onto the mat.

'Whatever is the matter, Edith?'

'Oh, I'm just being silly.'

'Tell me, what can I do?'

'Well, you could start by sharing a cuppa with me, then we can watch the soaps.'

'I'm sorry, but I haven't got that long.'

'No, dear. I know, but you really ought to see what that lovely girl, you know the one I mean, with the hair . . .'

I let Ms Smythes, Edith, as she keeps reminding me, lead the conversation. The soaps are her only link to the outside world she finds increasingly difficult to approach. The current story taking precedence over Coronation Street is discussed at length as though the actors are family. The news comes next, but she doesn't notice my concentration waver when the presenter mentions a familiar name. By the time she's finished talking, I've completely lost the thread of the conversation and offer to boil the kettle for her second cup of tea, pouring my own, now cold and coated with a film of cream, down the sink.

'Something on your mind?' she says.

'Don't you worry about me.'

'Well I do, you know. You're here to look after me. You look tired.'

Her dull grey eyes, blurred by cataracts quiz me. I can't fall apart in front of a client so I do what I always do, and divert the conversation.

I turn towards the kitchen window and glance down at the ground where burnt orange and cinnamon coloured leaves have fallen. 'Autumn is on its way.'

But she dismisses my comment and continues to steer me towards self-disclosure.

'I know when something's the matter with all my girls.' My age is meaningless. To her, I will always be a girl.

I shake my head before the images begin to resurface. 'You look tired.'

I am tired. Tired of lying. Tired of having to control everything. Tired of having nobody to confide in.

Has Steven noticed the dark circles beneath my eyes?

She hauls herself out of the chair and turns towards the kettle. 'I'll make the tea. You sit down, and we'll have a nice chat.'

She looks hopeful I'm going to unload some of my baggage onto her, but I know that's not going to happen. I was taught early on to retain an emotional distance with my clients. Besides, I cannot off-load such intimate details of my life to Ms Smythes. Nobody should have to hear *that*.

'I've got another call to make.'

'I understand.'

But I don't think she does.

'Maybe next time.'

'Sure.'

I leave the house, jump into the car, twist the key in the ignition, leaving a plume of smoke to trail after me, and sending grit to hit against the lower body of the car. As I glance into the rear-view mirror to catch Ms Smythes stood in the doorway, I speed off.

I haven't run away in years. In the early days of our marriage, I'd often drive for miles in no particular direction, usually finding myself far from home. Unable to recall how I'd got there, I used to pretend I'd gone in search of something. A place to take the children on the weekend. But, really, I think, although I can't be sure, I was searching for the missing part of myself. A piece that had been stolen without consent.

When I open my eyes, or at least that's how it feels - like I've been asleep - I notice a sign declaring: welcome to Gloucestershire.

TERESA

I hadn't expected this day to come. Not for years. Perhaps never.

'What's her name?'

'Emma.'

'And how old is she?'

'My age.'

'And where does Emma, aged sixteen live?'

'In Southmead.'

My jaw stiffened. Why couldn't he find himself a nice girlfriend, one who lived closer.

'The council estate?'

He shook his head.

'Her dad's a doctor and her mother's a teacher at the Ministry Of Defence school. They live in Twenty Acres.'

The estate wasn't rough, but it was working class. Comprising several buildings given to MOD workers at the cusp of where Southmead met Brentry. The school was situated at the lower end of the estate. Convenient and close to the shops where thugs hung out until late. I guessed with parents like her's Antony hadn't met them.

'You'd get on with her mum. She's really relaxed.'

Euphemism for lazy.

'And what does Emma do?'

'She's studying English. She wants to meet you. I said you'd cook tonight.'

'I really don't think-'

'Mum, it's only dinner.'

'Fine.'

I both loved and loathed Antony's tendency towards assumption. His world was simple. A stable playing field where routine took precedence over reality. Where I would always be there for him and he'd remain forever a child. But even *he* must have known to a certain extent how damaging such a belief would be.

I was reluctant to agree to Emma's visit but felt backed into a corner.

'Wouldn't it be better if she came Saturday? I haven't got enough food in.'

'I borrowed some money off dad.'

'That's, lovely. But . . .'

'For fucks sake, mum.'

'You could rent a film from Blockbusters if you wait.'

'Whatever.'

He strode from the room, knocking a vase of flowers to the ground, the petals already decayed crisp underfoot as I collected the broken porcelain from the floor.

Since Dominic's release, Antony's anger had increased, though I rarely had to contend with it alone, for he spent most of his time with Nathan going on bike rides. Most evenings, come rain or shine, they'd cycle together from Lockleaze, as far as Avonmouth or Fishponds, following the track through Easton, ending in St. Philips causeway.

I drove past them once. I'd been shopping in the new fruit market. Antony, Dominic, and Nathan were stood at one end of the street, their bikes leaning against a wall, oblivious that several yards away I watched them talking to two young girls. At the time, I was shocked they'd cycled so far and considered offering them a lift. But when I saw they were engrossed in conversation, I decided they wouldn't appreciate my interruption. I didn't want to appear overbearing so I continued on my way. Only now, I've begun to question how solid my recall of this event is.

Were the girls smiling beneath the shade or were their faces overshadowed with concern?

When I stopped at the junction beside the bridge, glancing down at the river below, suddenly feeling unsettled, had it been a premonition of things to come?

When I glanced up at the rear-view mirror to see Antony lean towards the girl who held her hand out against his chest, was she afraid of kissing in public or was it a distress signal?

I thought the girl was infatuated with Antony, but I could tell, even from behind the windscreen, twenty feet from her, she was far too young.

I never thought age was a problem back then. Antony was fifteen. The girl must have been around thirteen years old. Despite never hearing him mention her name in front of me, I guessed they'd fallen out when a few nights later I heard him crying in his room. I crept on tip-toes and stood, peering through the crack in the door. In the dim glow of a lamp, I caught him slumped forwards staring at his hands, shaking his head.

'I thought she liked me,' he said.

He often spoke to himself in order to make sense of something that troubled him. To any other parent the emotion-packed self-speech might cause them to shove the door open and demand to know what was the matter, but I'd dealt with far more pressing issues when it came to my son so it wasn't until recent events forced me to re-evaluate things that I began to wonder why the girl had dumped him.

Antony blocked real conversation. He put up a wall of defence between us after his father re-appeared in his life, and if I thought I struggled to understand him before, there was no hope of rekindling the false relationship I prided us having then. Because of course, it had never existed. I dismissed any concerns that arose over the coming months as hormone related.

When Antony approached me and confided having eyes on someone, telling me they couldn't be together, I didn't think to question why.

'She wouldn't want to be with me.'

'Rubbish. You're a handsome lad. Okay, perhaps you could lose a few pounds, but you can be kind and loving. Any woman would feel lucky if you asked them on a date.'

'You think?'

'I know we've had our differences, but that's because when you were younger I struggled to understand you. You're not like other boys your age. You're sensitive. Women love that.'

He seemed surprised by my reaction.

'What you need to do is be honest with her. Tell her how you feel. Ask her to go with you to the cinema or something.'

'Dad said he'd give me some money on the weekend. He said I'm old enough to respect it now.'

'Well, there you are then. Spend it wisely and enjoy yourself.'

'I'll take her out Saturday.'

I nodded.

He thanked me in his way. He came close to hugging me. A few times I'd made the first move but it had always sent him reeling backwards in shock. You see, he never knew what to do with affection. He felt love. Of that I was sure. But he struggled to express it. That day though, he came right up to me so that I could smell the deodorant his father had bought him, telling him he was a man now and had to act like one. He looked as though he wanted to be held, but I knew the moment I stepped towards him an awkward dance would ensue, and I didn't have time. I had washing to do.

I'll never know what happened. I heard from Antony in broken words streaked with tears, that he'd planned to take Catherine out to the cinema followed by fish and chips whilst they gazed at the stars. The girl had clearly broken his heart and that night, cradling him as he wept, repeating her name over and over- 'Kat, my Kat,' it was obvious he felt more for her than she did him.

His experiences with dating had left huge dents in his heart. First, Emma. Then Catherine. Knowing he was ready for a girlfriend, I thought it appropriate to talk to him about taking precautions. I knew only too well how devastating an unplanned pregnancy was and I didn't want Antony making the same mistake I had.

Of course, I was married and almost twenty-two when I'd fallen pregnant with Antony, but being a lone mother was incredibly difficult in the sixties and seventies. People looked down on me. I heard mothers in the playground whisper the word "slut" a few times, knowing it was aimed at me. Men ran the moment I mentioned the dreaded word- mother.

There had been men, of course. Discrete liaisons in the backs of cars or at home while Antony was at school. Some of them handsome, some of them with money, but none of them prepared to take on another man's child. Although, in hindsight, I guess they weren't prepared to sacrifice their marriages for me. A few of them had children of their own, and once or twice they'd accidentally come across Antony in the middle of the night on their way to the toilet or to fetch a glass of water. The ones who met him asked what was wrong with him, but I tried to downplay his problems. I used to say he was autistic. One of them, I forget his name now, told me his boy was artistic too. I can laugh about it now, but at the time, it wasn't a joke. Because of Antony, no man wanted to stick around. I was destined to be alone.

Talking of art, Antony enjoyed drawing. Aside from the games console it was the only thing that kept him occupied before Nathan and Dominic dug their claws into him. His portraits were mainly of animals and women. There was one in particular I liked. It was a sketch he'd made in the park one day after school while he waited for Nathan, who was always running late. I found the drawing under his bed, thinking it had fallen. I now wonder if he'd hidden it from me. Had he known then, his actions weren't considered normal?

The portrait was drawn in pencil. The girl had a beautiful innocence about her. She couldn't have been any older than nine or ten years of age. I assumed he'd seen the girl in the park that day, but when I asked about her, he just stared at the wall.

What would he have told me had I pressed him on it?

Would I have been able to prevent the route Antony took or was his future already mapped out for him?

Had that been my final opportunity to ensure Antony did not grow up to become a nonce, obliterated in the blink of my ignorant eyes?

DI SILVER

Locke stands back from the computer and sighs. 'She knew about Antony's problem. Why else go to the trouble of giving us a false address?'

I'm more pissed off that we didn't check it out before we left her. If we'd have known then that 63 Carlton Drive was a factory we would have been able to stop her from leaving.

'I knew she was hiding something. It was written all over her face.'

'Can we charge her for withholding information?'

'We've got to find her first.'

'I'll speak to the Super.'

KATE

I've driven almost thirty miles away. Further than I've ever gone during a complete memory lapse. I struggle to undo my seatbelt, my legs shake as I step out of the car, and fumble with the key as I attempt to lock the door. With no recollection of where I've been or what I've done, for all I know I could have driven into someone.

Could it be a symptom of my recent tranquilliser withdrawal? The side-effects are quite chilling if you read the little slip of paper stuffed inside the box so I try not to. It's somehow worse knowing what negative things might happen if I suddenly stop taking them, and far easier to deny their strength if I pretend their use is normal- like popping paracetamol.

I haven't been to Cirencester for years.

I round the corner past a small newsagents and walk the familiar route towards my childhood home. I was brought up here on a farm. The little crooked fence has been replaced with a four-foot high wall of grey stone, and the swinging gate is no longer there, leaving space for a driveway. My father never owned a car so there was no need for it back in those days.

The house appears smaller than my inner child remembers. The net curtains covering the windows are bright white and fancy. Nothing like my mother's. The place looks homely. Loved.

I prefer it this way, with the new red slate tiled roof, the careful segregation of chickens from the front garden covered in potted plants and LED lights on sticks.

A man crosses the road, looks at me with curiosity and turns into a house at the end of the road as though he's forgotten something. I walk back to the car and sit behind the wheel wondering if I've done this before. I recognise the house as it is now so come to the conclusion that I must have been here recently. Had the man seen me before or was he just curious to see a stranger stand rooted in front of his neighbours house, staring at it.

I turn the car deciding to turn a blind eye to the many possibilities racing through my skull and head back to Bristol.

The sky has grown dark, but the late Summer warmth remains as I turn into the street. I sit and stare at the house, noticing the downstairs lights are on, wondering what Steven will say when I enter hours later than usual.

The dashboard reads 9:15pm. I left Cirencester an hour ago. It takes forty minutes to drive from Ms Smythes' to Cirencester. So where the hell had I been for three hours since leaving her house?

Steven sits at the table reading this morning's newspaper as I enter the dining room. He looks up at me with weary eyes. 'I was trying to get hold of you.'

'I haven't checked my phone, but the signal is pretty bad over-'

He pats the chair beside him. 'Sit down.'

Steven isn't the kind of man to get angry and throw accusations at me. He's so laid back I often joke that he's horizontal, which is why I'm not prepared for the tone he uses.

'You're keeping things from me. You switched your phone off. I've no idea what's going on in your head at the moment but it stops right now. I want you to be honest with me. I can't take any more of your secrecy. I won't let you lie to me, Kate.'

My legs begin to quiver. Before I start to sway I place my handbag down onto the wooden cabinet where we keep the vintage plates stacked high for guests to use when or if they visit, and fall onto the seat.

'What are you keeping from me?'

I thought I'd been holding it together pretty well until today. I doubt he can sense my inner turmoil, so I'm guessing it's something else. But what?

'I don't know what you're talking about.'

'I can see it in your eyes. I know when you're lying.'

His hand falls inside the pocket of his trousers where he retrieves a half-empty pill packet, placing it on the table in front of me.

'I found these.'

'I haven't been using any more than usual.'

'You never told me why you'd been taking them at all. In fact, I'm starting to think you've been keeping things from me for some time because this is the second packet of Valium I've found in the last month which means you've been taking them every day recently.'

'Actually, I haven't taken any in two days.'

'Only because you've run out.' He sighs. 'I think you've become addicted to them.'

'They help me sleep. This past week, I've been finding it hard to, that's all.'

'Why?'

'Why what?'

'We've never spoken about your little accident since it happened, have we.'

'My *little accident* has got nothing to do with this.'

'If it's just insomnia then why hasn't your doctor offered you alternatives? Lavender oil is very good for sleep problems, or-'

'Steven, that won't work!'

'Does the Valium cause the sleep-walking?'

'The what?'

'You seem to be searching for something. I found you . . . can't you remember? You were trying to open the bedroom window. I can't bear to think what might have happened had I not woken up.'

'I don't sleep-walk. This is madness. There is nothing wrong with me. I'm fine.'

'Don't shut me out.'

'I'm not. There's nothing wrong with me.'

'Why don't you make an appointment with the doctor. I'm sure he could get you a referral to the sleep clinic. You can't take these forever,' he says, flipping the pill packet around in his hand.

'Lots of people struggle to sleep. The tablets help me and I don't take them every night, so what's the problem?'

'The problem is, Kate. I don't think you're being honest with me and I can't stand it anymore,' he says, pressing his finger lightly against my head. 'I need to know what is going on in there.'

'I've had enough.'

I jump from the chair and turn to leave. Steven holds out a hand, blocking my exit. He stands in front of the door. 'Please talk to me Kate.'

Rooted to the floor, breath tightening in my throat, Steven's words now inaudible through the thumping in my skull, I open my mouth to scream, but no sound comes out.

'What's the matter?'

My body is frozen, my voice gone.

'What is it?'

'I . . . I can't . . .'

'Sit down.'

'No.'

'Kate, please sit down. Something's wrong.'

'You . . . you can't make me do anything!'

My limbs are made of lead. I feel myself falling, crashing to the ground. A pain in my head. Black. Swimming. Sinking. Down I go into the pit of hell I've been trying desperately to hide from.

TERESA

I found the magazine under his bed. I was still shocked to discover Antony was ready for a relationship that might involve sex so when the photograph landed on the floor my heart beat faster. What fell from the pages of the magazine was the face of a young girl. Not just any girl, but the very girl he'd drawn. The name of the printers we used was stamped on the back of it. Having a camera in those days was a luxury so I was more concerned with how he'd afforded to pay for the film to be developed until I began rooting through his things.

I'm not sure what possessed me to enter his room uninvited that day, but had begun to wish I hadn't when I found the rest. Perhaps even then, I didn't trust him.

The guilt I felt over my discovery overshadowed all rational thought. I knew, somehow, I had to protect him. There was clearly something wrong with him.

The young girl in the photograph had her head cocked to one side, looking at someone or something in the distance. She didn't appear to be aware that anyone was snapping pictures of her.

I found the rest in his bookcase hidden between the pages of his favorite fantasy novels. I turned the place upside down then because my intuition was telling me that there was something very wrong about all of this, but the force of my denial was too strong to comprehend what it was.

The rest of the photographs confirmed my suspicions. In none of them was she facing the camera. In one she was playing with another girl, her image blurred as the lens remained focused on the youngest girl. I couldn't see in her what Antony found so compelling. I had no idea when the photographs had been taken but assumed it was not long after Christmas the year before. There was still a healthy dose of snow on the ground in one corner of the playing field. Which meant that Antony had used his own camera, a present from his father. I recognised the swings in the background. The photographs were taken in the playing field where Antony often met Nathan and Dominic before taking off on an expedition with their bikes.

You could see the flair of artistry he used to capture her. In some the girl had her back turned to the camera, her hair flung away from her face by the wind. There was no eroticism in them. They were more of an experimentation of his skills. He was a keen photographer. At least that's what I told myself when I decided not to mention them to anyone.

I should have listened to my instinct. It was screaming out at me to take notice, but when it's your own child, the boy you've raised on your own, the young man you've witnessed developing into a handsome teenager, maturing into an adult, you don't think about *those* things. You don't want to.

But, like I said, the warning signs were there. Central to his later involvement with the police. Apparently, they suspected nothing. Nobody did. Least of all me. But if I'm to be honest, I have to say that I always knew it would come to this: visiting my son behind bars. I used to pray that it wouldn't be for anything too serious. After all, he'd left home years ago, he'd got married and had a child of his own. He seemed to have it all: a nice safe job, a good enough income, both parent's still alive to turn to if he needed us. Now all of that has gone. He has no-one. I'm no longer viewed as the mother, but the enabler. The woman who allowed her son to get away with too much when he was young. I caused him to become the man he is. If anyone is to blame for his actions, it is I.

But they're wrong.

DI SILVER

The call comes in just as I'm about to hang up my coat. A female body was discovered lying at the foot of the stairs in her apartment at 7:30 this morning. The woman matches the description of Sophie Anderson. Dawson tells me that the SOCO has confirmed her death is being treated as suspicious.

'The pathologist believes she's been dead for at least twenty-four hours. If it wasn't for the postman having trouble fitting that parcel through the letterbox, who knows how long she'd have been there before someone discovered her?'

'What have they said regarding the weapon?'

'Nine-inch blade. Probably kitchen, used for meat.'

'Where are you going?' says Dawson, catching me in the act of flinging on my coat.

'Thought we'd take a look at the CS analysis Serg.'

'Blake and Flint are at the crime scene. I'd like you here. Keep an eye on the interviews for the Eastville Attacker.'

'Serg,' Locke nods, raising her eyes to the sky. She sighs. 'A woman's work is never done.'

'Are you giving me my cue?'

'I've got it here, you go.'

'You sure?'

She's barely got time to answer before I turn and head

for the door.

It isn't until parking up alongside the Clifton apartment to witness Sophie's body being carried on a stretcher by two white-suited Crime Scene Analysts and into the private ambulance do I question whether spending the remainder of the morning filing paperwork would have been preferable.

KATE

My hands shake so much I almost tip the glass of water Steven has shoved in front of me all over my lap. He looks at me with tired eyes.

Do I detect sadness or confusion behind his weak smile?

'How are you feeling now?'

'Okay,' I stutter between chattering teeth.

'It might be a side-effect of the medication.'

'It's not,' I try to re-assure him, but he doesn't look as though he believes me.

'I really think you ought to see someone. It's not normal to keep fainting.'

Have I fainted in front of him before?

'Steven, I'm really okay. I'm tired and a little stressed that's all.'

He looks away, trying to hide his irritation.

I hold out my hand for him to pull me up from the floor. When I stand, I feel my head and look down at the tiny spots of blood from the cut above my eye.

'I'll get you a plaster.'

The urge to run is over-powered by fear. Steven's worried voice crossing the distance between the images swooping past my eyelids: a bare mattress, my knickers discarded on the floor, the sound of a dog barking downstairs, the loud beat of the Sex Pistols coming from the cassette player. . .

Steven returns and leads me into the living room, easing me onto the sofa, pulling my legs up so that I'm lying back on the cushion he's placed behind my head.

Sitting beside me he looks at the floor.

'I know there's more. I know you're finding it hard to talk to me about it, whatever *it* is. But, I hope you realise that until you face it head-on it will go on destroying you. You have to let it go.'

He pauses, hoping I'll fill in the silence, breathing in a lungful of air before he continues.

'Keeping things from each other is only going to drive a further wedge between us. I love you, Kate. I want you to be happy. That's all I've ever wanted.'

I turn away so he can't see the single tear falling down one side of my face.

'I love you too.'

'How can I help you if you don't share it with me?'

I shake my head. 'It's not that easy.'

I try to retract my words, but Steven looks at me with relief.

'I knew there was something.'

'Steven-'

'I couldn't bear to lose you.'

I look up at him, noting the fear in his eyes.

'Steven, I've never betrayed you. I've only ever loved you.'

He senses that what I was about to say is another fabricated version of the truth. He jumps up from the sofa and heads for the door. I run after him.

'Steven?'

He snatches his coat from the hook and opens the

front door.

'Steven, wait!'

The thought of losing him is worse than telling him the truth.

I'm about to get up to pour myself a glass of wine, to numb down the sinking feeling of having argued with Steven for the first time in months over something so trivial as my sleeping problems when I hear his car crawl up to the pavement at the front of the house. He walks slowly towards the front door, pausing in the porch, planning what he will say to me before he enters.

But he shouldn't be the one to apologise. I should have told him right from the start. I've been a closed book for too long. But that's about to change because in the two hours I've sat here with only the sound of my breath and the monotonous ticking of the clock for company, I've realised how lonely and cold my life would be without him in it, and I don't ever want it to be that way.

He walks towards the living room noticing my hands pressed together on my lap as if in prayer. He stands in the doorway gauging the atmosphere for hostility or anger. When he finds none he makes his way over to the chair facing the TV.

I lean forward, removing the remote control from his hand. He stares down at his empty palm and brings his eyes up to meet mine.

'I don't want to fight.'

'Me neither.'

There is a beat of silence whilst I decide on the best

way to tackle the conversation. It will be one of the hardest I've had to begin. But no worse than speaking to those detectives, I tell myself.

'You're right.'

He moves back in his seat as if he's been hit with something.

'Antony.'

'Wh . . . what did you say?'

'Antony. That's his name, isn't it?'

I sit there stunned.

'You called his name out in bed.'

'What, when?'

'Last night.'

'In my sleep?'

He nods.

'Steven . . .'

'How long have you been with him?'

'No. It's not like that.'

'Was it just the once or . . .'

'I have been keeping something from you, and it's time I told you the truth. But I want you to promise me that you will let me tell you everything without interruption, otherwise I don't think I'll be able to finish.'

'I don't think I can-'

'Please, Steven. It's not what you think.'

He opens his mouth to say something but thinks better of it.

His jaw tightens, his eyes narrow. He turns to face the door.

'I thought I could forget about what happened and pretend that nothing came before us, but I've realised that's impossible. There are some things that are so difficult to put into words it's harder to speak them than to live with the trauma.'

I try to steady my breathing, hoping to bide my time against the inevitable discussion I know could make or break us.

'It was a hot day. I'd gone to meet some friends . . .'

My mind wanders back to that blistering Summer afternoon in the park. I allow the images to unfold before me, taking me back to the moments that changed my life forever.

'My mum was always telling me to turn the stereo down. She hated punk music. I guess that's why I did it. The rebel in me always won out. If I'd have taken a different route home, if I'd have listened to my mum for once it might never have happened.'

Steven holds out his hand sensing that what I'm about to impart is something huge; much bigger than Antony.

I shake my head.

'I don't want your pity. I know what I did was wrong, but it was never spoken about then. People used to leave their front doors unlocked. Nobody thought anything bad was going to happen to them. People were more trusting. Being vigilant meant checking the weather. I guess the signs were there, but back then, nobody knew what they were, or even thought to look. I don't blame my parents. I was very good at hiding it.'

I continue off-loading my story in the hope that it will allow me to release the stranglehold I have over the past because I know that deep down I've been gripping onto it too tightly for fear that if I let it go I'll be losing a part of myself. Despite how much pain it causes me, it's comforting having a secret like this. I'm used to it. The familiar isn't as frightening as the unknown. Releasing it had always been a terrifying prospect.

I picture myself laughing, my blonde hair glinting in the sunlight emanating through the window. My tanned waif-like hand reaching out to hit the buttons on the tape recorder. The flat in Lockleaze. The pulsing beat of punk music clattering out of the speakers in the dusty stereo. A can of beer. Antony's friendly eyes trailing down the small curves of my blossoming figure.

I shudder with the knowledge of a forty-four-year-old at what he must have been thinking when he looked at me like that.

My eyes flit briefly towards Steven before skittering away again. He searches through his confusion for a hint as to what my story could possibly tell him about my troubled sleep, recent fainting fit, or Antony.

'I trusted him.'

Steven's broad shoulders straighten up.

'I was fourteen.'

'He took advantage of you?'

I break down before I can answer.

TERESA

I leave the car outside the prison, making my way towards the ominous looking building. There is a small queue of men, several of them holding a briefcase. A couple of worried looking women wait to meet with their client, spouse, or son. The grey building houses hundreds of men, all accused of crimes similar to Antony. As I near the door a tall stocky man tells me to stand aside as a female prison officer with short dark hair searches through my bag. The security guard asks me to step forwards so that he can wave a security device shaped like a wand over me. The scanner beeps, he nods, steps back and allows me through.

At the desk, I give over the name of the prisoner I'm visiting before another female prison officer escorts me down a narrow hall and in through a set of double doors.

The room is dim, despite the strip lights in the ceiling and the wide bullet-proof windows lining one wall. Several small tables are nailed to the floor, two plastic chairs at either side of them. The smell of testosterone fills the air I share with fifteen men who sit as still as corpses. Antony sits staring at the shiny surface of the grey melamine table in front of him. His gaze doesn't waver as I take the seat opposite. Anyone else would think his inability to meet my eyes convicts him, but it's not guilt I see in them. It's shame.

I glance around the room searching for something to say. I speak just to break the uncomfortable silence.

'I'm glad they didn't send you too far.'

When he doesn't respond I continue.

'I saw Hannah at the weekend. She says she can't visit because of the little ones, but she hopes to see you soon.'

He looks at me then.

'She believes you're innocent.'

He nods and returns his gaze to the table.

'How are you coping?'

I shuffle in my seat.

'Don't you want to speak to your mother?'

His eyes fill with tears.

'I didn't do those things.'

'The evidence is quite compelling.'

I don't mean to appear so flippant, but what does he want me to say? He's being charged with one of the most horrendous crimes, and yet, he sits there looking washed-out. Like he's given up already.

I lean towards him and lower my voice.

'Is it some kind of compulsion that you can't control?'

He leaps back and jumps from his seat.

'I didn't do it!'

'Sit down.'

The male prison officer stood in the entrance comes towards us, tells Antony to calm down, and glowers at me.

'Antony, please?'

He resumes his position on the seat, dropping his head.

'I have a wife, a daughter. I shouldn't be here.'

'What did you say during your interview?'

He looks at me as though I've asked him the most ridiculous question.

'I love Jacky, I would never cheat on her.'

'You haven't been sent here for an affair, Antony.'

I catch myself laughing. Noticing the female prison officer looking at me, I stop. I don't want to give them the impression I'm happy to be here. I'm sure she knows who Antony is. It's been years since he left the music scene, but nobody could forget his face. One of three members of a punk band they named themselves, Blue Wave.

Antony's choice in music was limited to The Sex Pistols and The Clash. In his late teens the walls of his bedroom were plastered with posters of them. At the age of eighteen, six foot tall, with a mop of almond coloured hair, and handsome features he'd inherited from his father he seemed to have it all. He worked at a record shop, at the bottom of Gloucester Road, spending all his free time practicing lyrics with Nathan and Dominic. Antony wasn't very good at remembering chords so he took over as lead singer. They had a decent following and a few groupies, often young girls who attended all their gigs at the local pubs and festivals.

I don't know what happened to their dreams of taking over the world, but in the Summer of 1987 Nathan gave up the drums and Dominic hung up the electric guitar to find more suitable regular work. Antony being more hands-on and terrible at spelling, gave up song writing and applied, with my assistance to take an engineering course at the local college. Two years later he began working at the aerospace manufacturers. He'd been working there until his redundancy six months ago when he secured a job as a minibus driver for the local school.

Antony's voice intrudes on the memory.

'I didn't touch her.'

'The one who's agreed to go to the papers when the trial is over?'

'No. Sophie. I didn't, mum. I wouldn't.'

'She lied?'

I desperately want to believe him. I know it's stupid of me to doubt the police, the Crown Prosecution Service and the systems they have in place which aim to protect young girls from men like him, but what if Antony is telling the truth?

I know him better than anyone. I know that right now, looking into his eyes, he genuinely believes he is being truthful. But our beliefs are subjective, aren't they? He might not realise the things he is being accused of were wrong acts to commit.

'I can only help you if you're honest with me.'

'She thought I had money so she made it up.'

'You think she wanted a payout?'

'I know she did. She told me she wanted to leave home, and I told her that I'd help her.'

'She was running away?'

'She said her dad hurt her. She wanted to get away from him. It was the only way she knew how.'

'But, you should've known that it would cause trouble. Helping a young girl to escape her parents is still wrong.'

'Not when she was being molested.'

I jolt backwards in shock.

'You mean you were *helping* Sophie?'

'That's what I told them, but they don't believe me.'

This changes everything.

'And Emma, what happened with her?'

'She dumped me. She said she didn't want to date a virgin.'

'What about the other woman?'

'I never even met her.'

'Antony, you need to explain to your solicitor that this has all been a huge mistake.'

'I already have. Even *he* says I should plead guilty for a lesser sentence.'

'Then you need another one. Let me find you someone with more experience, a good reputation. We need to get you out of here. This is no place for an innocent man.'

'It's not so bad. I have privileges that other prisoners don't get because I'm on remand.'

'I don't care. I want my boy home with his family where he belongs.'

It isn't until later, sat in the car staring through the windscreen at the other inmate's relatives leaving the building that I realise throughout our conversation Antony never once asked after his father.

I should have told Christopher as soon as he was arrested. But how do you voice such a statement? *Your only son is awaiting trial for this awful crime against a woman, do you want to come and see him?* Yes, I'm sure he'd love to learn of Antony's arrest in such a blasé fashion.

Back home I settle down in my favorite jade green chair, listening to the birdsong through the open window, and

I'm instantly transported back to the moment I waved Antony off to boarding school.

I stood staring at the ornamental pond that centred the acres of grassland. I'd been struggling to cope with Antony's temper for a long time, but he'd begun to lash out at the slightest thing. His school had suspended him several times that Summer, after which I was invited into the headteacher's office. Mr Jones was concerned over Antony's lack of educational progress and recommended spending six months in a highly regarded residential school for boys.

These days you would expect your child to attend a mainstream school with special provision for behavioural, social, emotional and learning difficulties, but in those days Antony's behaviour was deemed a nuisance. At the age of thirteen Antony was a reclusive boy, but when he returned he'd been dragged out of his shell for the worse. There were some positives though. Time away from Antony gave me the breathing space I needed during the week so that I was able to keep my job at the launderette. I met Caroline once I was able to make friends and socialise.

On one of Antony's weekend visits home, I introduced him to Caroline, thinking he'd be pleased to have another adult around. She was a year older than me and had two grown boys of her own. Their father refused to allow her contact so I never met them. I hadn't thought myself that way inclined until I found myself staring into her bright blue eyes. Something I couldn't describe fizzled between us until she made the first move. It felt good. Comfortable.

That weekend, Antony met her for the first time and

without his blessing Caroline moved into the house a few days later. Antony remained in boarding school until the following July, six months longer than he'd expected.

I had absolutely no idea what they'd done to him in there but he reverted back to the shy, distant child he'd been before the hormones kicked in. Of course, it would take me years to discover that he'd been afflicted with such awful discipline that he'd developed a hatred of the establishment and would never again view the system which now incarcerated him with respect. Because of the beatings he endured in the school, he developed a fondness for loud punk music. This time, the screaming he'd forced on my ears as a child now rhymed. The lyrics were, I believe, aimed at releasing his anger and frustration with a world that didn't seem to understand him or care to try.

I'm jolted back to the present by the sound of someone hammering on the door.

A woman wearing a light cream suit over a bright pink blouse stands in the doorway. She wears the same shade of pink on her lips and speaks with a tight-lipped upper-class accent.

'Jennifer Tate.'

The defence solicitor I've enlisted for Antony.

'Come in.'

I called her on my way home from HMP Ashfield as I sat in front of the steering wheel, my hand shaking as I tried to decide who I should call first: Christopher or the woman whose number I found on the internet. I decided on the latter. Christopher could wait.

I invite her into the living room. She takes a seat beside me, clutching her briefcase tight against her thin lap.

'I mentioned earlier I'm on a tight schedule so if you don't mind I'd like you to give me a brief low-down of the case, and I'll tell you how I can help.'

I nod my head in agreement.

'First, I need your son's name?'

'Antony Christopher Wells.'

'Date of birth?'

'The eighth of August 1967.'

'What offences has he been charged with?'

'Obtaining indecent images of children and one count of . . .' I swallow back the bile that clogs my throat. 'Rape.'

'How is he pleading?'

'Not guilty.'

She pauses, straightens up, and looks at me as if gauging my reaction.

'Does he have a police record?'

'Minor offences when he was younger.'

'What were they in connection with?'

'Theft, driving a stolen motorbike without a licence or insurance, and . . .'

I have no idea how to explain this one.

She offers me a flaky warm smile in the hope that I will continue quickly. I get the impression from the way she stares at me that the conversation is about to become more brutal. I feel like a traitor to my son.

'Arson.'

'How long ago were these offences indicted?'

'I'm sorry?'

'When was he charged with committing the offences, Ms Carter?'

'He was thirteen when he set fire to the boarding school. One of the teachers had beaten him with a ruler. He came home covered in bruises. It knocked his confidence. I'd spent so long trying to bring him out of himself then-'

'Let's stick to the facts shall we, Ms Carter?'

I'm slightly wounded by her forthright manner. Not being able to explain why Antony's final act of violence had been both the reason for his exclusion from boarding school and the cause of his sudden interest in music sets my heart racing in irritation.

'I really think you need to listen-'

'If I wish to take your son on as a client it will be my job to defend him. So there is one more question I'd like to ask before I can progress. It will help me to gain a clear perspective on which way to tackle the case.'

'Okay.'

'Is Antony innocent?'

Well, that's the penultimate question, isn't it?

Could Antony have raped a woman he claims to have never met? Did he abuse Sophie? Were the images found on his laptop downloaded by my son?

'Absolutely.'

DI SILVER

I divert my attention from the road towards Burger King, moaning when I realise the time on the dashboard.

The media frenzy over the Eastville Knifer takes precedence over my grumbling stomach.

Locke snakes her way towards the car as I turn into the forecourt. She tosses her cigarette and grinds it into the concrete, opening the door before I've released my seat belt.

'Any evidence on who killed her?'

I called Locke just before I left Sophie's.

'Nothing obvious.'

'No DNA, no fingerprints, no sign of a struggle?'

I shake my head. 'It looks like she knew her attacker and let him in.'

'What did the pathologist say?'

'Stab wound to the throat, sliced evenly.'

'No chance it was a suicide?'

'Doubtful.'

'I've found Jacky.'

'You have?'

'We're going there now.'

'But I haven't-'

'We'll grab some food on the way.'

We reach the Weston Road in forty minutes. A maze of traffic cones redirecting us adds several miles onto our journey so we stop into a supermarket en route.

'Happy now?' says Locke.

Unable to speak through the sandwich I've crammed into my mouth, I nod.

Jacky's sister lives in a large Victorian style abode with three cats, two scrawny looking dogs, and a pet lizard. It's the kind of home that makes my skin crawl, not from untidiness, but from a lack of sunlight.

'What's with this family, are they all vampires?'

Locke notices the closed curtains too.

'I'd bet you a tenner Jacky is a witch.'

As we near the front door where a pile of stones lie on the ground beside a mangy looking black cat, I can only nod my approval at her prediction.

'Donna Wilson?'

The thin, gaunt looking woman who greets us at the door looks as though sunlight is her nemesis too.

'Dialysis,' she says, leading us along the hall towards a light spacious kitchen diner.

Health problems must run in the family, I think, taking a look around the house to see Jacky outstretched on the sofa, the cushions sagging beneath her weight.

'Detectives,' she says, cocking her head to one side.

Is she mocking us or basking in the attention?

'Is there somewhere private we could go?'

'Garden,' she says, clambering off the sofa and escorting us through the back door which leads onto a patio garden that looks just as unkempt as the house.

'What do you want now? I've told you everything.'

'You could start by telling us why you gave us a false

address.'

'I wanted some peace. Got media outside my door every second of every bloody day.'

'We need some more information, Mrs Wells.'

'About what?'

'Your relationship with your husband.'

'Better make a pot of tea then 'adn't I.'

Locke follows her into the kitchen, keeping up idle chit-chat as I examine the area for a clue as to what kind of life her sister leads, but nothing untoward stands out.

When Jacky returns, taking up over half of the bench beside me, I see that Locke's hands rest in the pockets of her trousers and decide not to waste any more time.

'Did your husband ever give you a reason to suspect him of anything?'

'No.'

'Never pulled your hair in bed or hit your daughter?'

'No.'

'Did he ever ask you to dress up, call him daddy?'

'No.'

'So you had no idea he was using your phone to access porn sites depicting adult women dressed in school uniforms?'

'No.'

'You never suspected your husband had a fondness for sexual encounters with children?'

Stretching her head back to roll her eyes at the sky she eventually pipes up another, definite, 'no.'

'He's a sensitive man. Private. But I never thought he was into none of that.'

'And what do you think now, Mrs Wells?' says Locke, standing close enough to see the guilt emanating off

Jacky's sweat coated forehead.

'I don't believe it.'

'But you've left your marital home, haven't you?'

'I don't want to talk about it no more.'

'What does your daughter think? She's close to her father, isn't she?'

'He's been there for her since day one. Her biological father was a deadbeat. Never did nothing. Not paid a penny since she was born.'

'Antony's her step-father?'

'Don't say nothing, mind.'

'She doesn't know?'

She shakes her head. 'I'd like to keep it that way.'

Locke turns to me in the car. 'That's a turn up for the books.'

'So that's what she was hiding.'

'Makes you think though, doesn't it?'

I offer her a cursory glance of acknowledgement.

Makes you wonder what else she's hiding.

'Typical case of secrets and lies then.'

'Someone didn't want Sophie to talk. I wouldn't call anything about this case typical.'

'I mean Jacky. You know, wife gets bored of her average sex life, has an affair, Antony brings up the baby, oblivious. No wonder she didn't want to talk.'

'Average is subjective. Once a month for him might be considered normal.'

'I get the impression everything is too cut and dried.'

'I know what you mean,' says Locke, turning the car into the station.

'You think he was set up?'

'It would take a genius to get two women to accuse him of rape and give enough false information to secure a conviction.'

'Three.'

Locke shakes her head. 'Kate never gave a statement, and she didn't actually name him. The CPS think she's an unreliable witness.'

'What about Isla?'

'I've spoken to Johnno at the Met. He said they're having a hard time pinning anything on him as the evidence is circumstantial.'

'Sophie's death is rather convenient then.'

'Exactly.'

'What about the girl who didn't want to be interviewed?'

'Emma?'

'Yeah.'

'Closed down. Blake thinks she was a limelight snatcher.'

'So, what's gonna happen now?'

'Unless anyone else comes forward he'll be released tomorrow.'

'That soon?'

'He didn't share the videos.'

'He only downloaded them?'

She ignores the sarcasm in my voice and applies the handbrake.

KATE

I watch Steven sleeping beside me, snoring, content, and wonder if I'll ever experience a dreamless night without picturing Antony's cold hard stare as an image of my young, naked limbs send me racing from the bed, locking myself in the bathroom, my head over the toilet bowl.

Last night with my eyes cast to the floor, focused on a stain in the wood so I didn't have to see Steven's reaction as I recounted the day I met Antony and the abuse I endured for the following two years, almost seems like a long distant memory now.

Dawn forces the sun to peep up from the horizon, leaving a sour note to hang in the air between us. Even telling him the truth hasn't made it go away, if anything it's as raw as ever. Of course, I glossed over the details. I didn't want Steven to picture what made me the woman I am today.

After I told him, I couldn't look him in the eye. I had to decide how much to say by the way his hand shook. When he was motionless I had to gauge how far through the tunnel of hell to take him. The silence was deafening. When I did eventually dare to take a quick glance at his face, I noticed his eyes had glazed over and his nose was wet. He held his hand out for me to take, snatching it away the moment our skin touched.

Rubbing his hands over the rough fabric of his trousers, absentmindedly tearing at the fabric of his shirt sleeves. 'That evil . . .'

Numb, I hoped my lack of movement would calm him, but he was so focused on his own thoughts and feelings that he didn't notice me glide a nail across my wrist as I tread carefully over the horror until my throat was sore. Until my tears turned into heaving sobs. Until I could no longer imagine being back there, in that bedroom, but instead, felt as though I *was* there, reliving it.

Then more silence as he tried to absorb the words to make sense of them.

'I don't know what to say.'

'You don't have to say anything.'

'Thank you. I mean, for telling me.'

'You needed to know.'

'I guess I wasn't expecting anything like that.'

He twitched his eyebrows. He tensed his jaw. The lines on his forehead creased. He shook his head, running a hand through his hair.

'I could kill that . . . that . . . what he did.'

'I know you're upset, but-'

'Why didn't you give a statement to the police?'

'I couldn't go through with it. I was young. I didn't know how to deal with it.'

'You thought you could forget about it?'

I tried.

'Erase it from your head?'

I guess.

'I had my GCSE's coming up. I thought it would be the right thing to do.'

'Right for who?'

'For me.'

Steven left the sofa as though he'd been stung.

'Steven?'

'You've had to live with this for years, while he gets away with it.'

'No, he hasn't.'

He looked at me then with a single tear spilling free, falling down his left cheek.

'He's been arrested. They found pictures, videos on his phone. Two women came forward to say that he abused them.'

'Right.'

'It was on the news.'

'When?'

Steven rarely watches the news on TV during the week.

'Two weeks ago.'

'Why didn't you tell me?'

'I tried, but there never seemed to be a good time. It wasn't until the detectives showed up at the door that I realised I couldn't stand by and watch him . . . I had to say something.'

'You should have told me sooner. I'm your husband, Kate. I could have been there for you.'

I crossed the room towards him. 'You're here now. That's all that matters.'

'You let me think . . . oh God, I thought you were having an affair.'

The very idea is an insult.

'Why now?' he says, his tone sharpening with every breath.

'Because it's time I told the truth.'

'You said that the police came.'

'I told them some things.'

'What things?'

'I couldn't . . . I didn't-'

'You didn't tell them what happened to you?'

'And now it looks like the case is going to collapse.'

'Why?'

'Apparently, the first woman who came forward was . . . murdered. They think whoever killed her wanted to keep her quiet.'

Steven ran both hands through his hair and shook his head.

'This is huge. Dangerous.'

'I know.'

'Is that why you're telling me now?'

'No, Steven. It's been eating me up inside. If telling you is the only way I can start to deal with it properly then-'

'You said the first woman was killed. There were others?'

'Her case is different. Another force has been investigating it separately. And, she's agreed to give an interview to the press when the trial is over. It's not looking good.'

'They think she's doing it for the money?'

'Yes.'

'So her case might be deemed invalid?'

'Yes.'

'So they have no evidence to prosecute this man? They have nothing concrete to base their case on?'

'It's crumbling down around them.'

'Where does that leave you?'

'Even if I told them the truth, my statement could only be used as a declaration of victim impact.'

'So it wouldn't help the case against this man?'

'I doubt it.'

He shook his head. 'I don't know why you couldn't tell me. I understand you probably think you're to blame or something, but you shouldn't be ashamed of what happened. That filthy pervert is the one who should be ashamed, preying on innocent girls.'

'I don't want pity.'

'I don't know how to help you.'

'Just listen. Be there for me. That's all you can do.'

'This is too much.'

'I know.'

'I just can't believe you've been keeping all this stuff to yourself, and for so long.'

He shifted on his feet then turned towards the door.

'Where are you going?'

'I need to clear my head.'

'Steven?' *I need you.*

'I'm sorry. I . . . I need some air.'

I edge away from the bed, creeping along the carpet, stepping over the loose floorboard, praying he doesn't wake.

Steven appears in the kitchen a few minutes later as I stand with my back to him, stirring a fresh cup of coffee between bleary eyes.

I sense his gaze on the back of my neck, but when I turn he's gone.

I run to the window and watch him close the car door behind himself. Hunched over the steering wheel gripped tightly in his hands, head back, eyes closed, mouth open, he screams. He shouts. He rages. Releasing the pent up emotions I couldn't all those years ago.

I watch his shoulders relax, his hands fall down to his lap, his eyes tracing the fields in the distance, almost hidden behind thick layers of brick and mortar. When he punches the steering wheel, once, twice, I tear my eyes away from him. His pain and anger is too much for me to bear.

Whatever's going through his head is nothing compared to how shit I feel for lying to him for all these years. Still in my dressing gown, I run to the door and step outside into the biting chill of an early Autumn morning.

He looks up at me from behind the windscreen and shakes his head.

I continue towards the car. We have to deal with this together.

TERESA

Hannah calls just as I'm about to warm a croissant in the microwave.

'Mum's filing for a divorce.'

'I see.' But what I really want to say is, shouldn't he be considered innocent until proven guilty?

'You know how stubborn mum is. I know he didn't do the things those women accused him of. He's my father, I know him better than anyone. But that's not the reason she's giving. She says the neighbours are talking about her, behind her back. She's selling the house. She's having some kind of meltdown.'

'She should ignore what everyone's saying and keep her chin up.'

'We are still talking about mum, aren't we?' she laughs.

'Yes, you're right. When has Jacky ever taken advice from anyone?'

'Maybe if she starts the ball rolling she'll realise the mistake she's made and she'll let it go.'

'And if she doesn't?'

'There could be another wedding on the horizon.'

'I see. She still loves him?'

'Of course.'

'You don't give up on the people you propose to love. In sickness and in health.'

'Till death us do part.'

'For richer for poorer.'

I wonder if Jacky is doing this for the money? Royalties from his music are still a nice tidy regular sum used to redecorate, or for Jacky to go on a spending spree.

'Are you going to visit your father, he'd love to see you?'

'I will, nan. Once the press back off.'

I glance out of the window, seeing two heads bopping up and down as reporters try to get a good shot of the front door through a man-made hole in the bush. 'I don't think there's any chance of that happening soon.'

'How is he coping?'

'Not good.'

Truthfully, I don't know. There's no way of knowing everything about a person. Whatever happened between Antony and those girls is a mystery, just as Jacky's decision to give up on her husband so soon baffles me.

I know Antony is capable of causing hurt, I've seen it with my own two eyes. The bird and the goldfish weren't the only animals he killed. Antony smothered his pet hamster at the age of twelve as it attempted to wriggle out of his fat hands. And the fire that destroyed two rooms in the boarding school, caused, according to Antony by a moment of pure madness. A delusional state that could have killed several people, if the warden hadn't discovered the smoke so quickly. But, even *I'm* struggling to comprehend the details which have begun to emerge in the newspapers and on the local television regarding the offences Antony has supposedly carried out over the past thirty years.

'I've hired a defence solicitor for your father. She's very good. She's meeting with him tomorrow to go over his statement. She says there is every chance of a successful appeal on the charges due to the police allowing media coverage of the case before it has been tried in court.'

'Misconduct?'

'Something like that. You should speak to your mother. I'm sure she doesn't wish to act too rash. She needs to be there for him, to support him.'

'I'll try.'

'You must, Hannah. Your father is in pieces. That place is no good for him. He's at risk of all kinds of violence and you know how he deals with confrontation, especially with authority.'

She sighs, then says, 'I'll speak to her later.'

'Good girl. You know your father thinks the world of you. If his own daughter had no belief in him I don't know what he'd do.'

I put the phone down, deciding it's time I told Christopher. He deserves to know. Despite his reluctance to speak to Antony since their most recent argument, I'm obliged to be the one to inform him of his son's arrest.

I dial the number, hoping he doesn't answer, leaving me no choice but to explain everything via voicemail, but there's no such luck. He answers on the second ring.

'He's being charged with what?'

'Surely they have the news where you are?'

'I've just returned from Spain.'

'Well, I hope you enjoyed your holiday.'

He ignores the note of sarcasm in my voice.

'Antony needs you.'

'So it seems.'

'Aren't you going to visit him?'

'I've no intention of hearing what that little shit has to say. He's been trouble from the moment he was born, why do you think . . .?'

'What?'

He takes a deep breath.

'Why do you think I couldn't stay around?'

I feel as though I've been slapped in the face.

'Because you met that tart.'

'Tee, it had nothing to do with that *tart*, as you like to call her.'

'What are you saying?'

'Antony was so difficult.'

'I know.'

'I couldn't stand coming home to that wailing child and my miserable wife. I needed space.'

'So you shacked up with her?'

'Karen was a breath of fresh air from the squalid dull home I was forced to share with you and that brat-'

'That's quite enough, Christopher. He's your son and he needs his father now more than ever.'

'He should have thought about that before smashing up my wife's car, shouldn't he?'

'This isn't about her car, Christopher.'

'You're right. It's about those women whose lives he shit on all those years ago. It's about the world as it is today. Look what happened in Rochdale and Oxford, even Bristol? All those girls, all those secrets and cover-ups. Look what it's done to all those women. And the church, the abuse scandals and-'

'Christopher, are you going to see your son in prison

or not?'

'Haven't I made myself clear? I'm not going to support that brute. No fucking way.'

'You don't think he might be innocent, that he might not have done anything wrong at all?'

'This time, like all the other times he's refused to obey the law and the morals of the land? Really, Tee, are you asking me if I think my son has been wrongly accused?'

'I'm asking you to be there for him. To support him. To let him know that no matter what, he is your son and that you will stand by him.'

'Like you have?'

'I'm his mother.'

'Blood is thicker than water?'

'Of course.'

'Well, I'm sorry to burst your bubble Tee, but I'm not as naive as you are.'

'What's that supposed to mean? Didn't we always say that no matter what happened our child would always be able to rely on us?'

'That's not what I meant?'

'What did you mean then, because I'm struggling to understand. Surely you're not suggesting that there are conditions to unconditional love?'

'In this case, Tee, there is. You seem to be forgetting that we're products of circumstance. Conditioned by society.'

'You're blaming me for this?'

'I'm saying that something awful happened to him as a child and he's been conditioned to act a certain way towards others. He probably believes those girls enjoy it.'

'What are you saying that our boy was . . . was . . .?'

'Oh, open your eyes, Tee. You think that a few spankings lead our son to set fire to his teacher's bedroom?'

I'm lost for words.

'Antony was mentally scarred, physically abused by his teacher. He tried to kill him in one final act of revenge. On some level, I think Antony missed him when he was excluded and sent home to us. He developed a warped sense of who he was as he grew up. Didn't you ever find it strange that most of the children he hung out with were much younger than him? Didn't you ever question what happened between him and that girl?'

'Emma?'

'No, the other one. Sophie. Didn't you ever wonder why a teenage boy would want to play with a seven-year-old girl? Didn't you ever ask the neighbours why the family next door left so suddenly?'

I cling tightly to the phone, lowered to my chest, muffling Christopher's voice. But, no matter how much or little I knew, I don't deserve to be spoken to in this way, and by a man who feels disowning his son the moment he needs him most is an acceptable punishment.

'Tee, he smashed Karen's car up because she told him to close the bathroom door when he took a shower. He doesn't understand boundaries like you and me. Nobody knows what happened when Antony was alone with a young girl who couldn't comprehend what he was doing to her, least of all fight back. Men like that, they groom their victims. They make them feel special. They take advantage of their weaknesses, their age, their vulnerabilities. They prey on young girls to fulfil some deep-rooted void. They pretend to be their friend or boyfriend then they abuse them. That's what they do.'

I've sunken to the floor, my legs shaking too much to carry my slight framed body to the chair. I sit with my arms wrapped around my legs, holding onto myself for fear that if I let go I will disappear through a portal into an alternate universe where this conversation is normal.

'Tee, are you still there?'

My son. My beautiful, difficult little boy, a paedophile?

'No, no, no, no, no, no . . .'

Unable to hold it together any longer, I begin to sob. Wiping the snot from my nose with my hand as Christopher calls my name through the phone I've tossed onto the floor beside my feet.

I don't think I can move off the ground where I lie, my breath ragged, crying tears of shame at my son's unfortunate existence; unable to let go of the belief that if I hadn't given birth to such a monster that my own and those other poor women's lives would have remained untouched by the cruelty of our present situation.

I blame myself for not drowning him when I imagined doing so would prevent the mother ship from making me keep him when my depression reverted to a form of psychosis all those years ago. If I had then my life sentence for murder would have long ago completed. But those women will go on suffering for the rest of their lives. I have failed them. But I won't, I can't fail my son. I must help him.

Antony must be made aware that exposing the truth is

the right thing to do. He needs to know that what he has done wrong has not only affected his own family but the lives of those women. His actions have created a ripple effect; a tidal wave tearing through the community.

He must plead guilty. It's the only way of saving those poor women from any further upset. They shouldn't have to speak out in court, being questioned over their memory, choice of clothing, potential promiscuity. One of the girls was a child when he had sex with her. She did nothing to provoke him. He chose to abuse her. He made the decision to rape her. He is the one who should suffer, they've spent far too many years torturing themselves with what if's and why's.

I should know. I've been doing it too. Only for other reasons. Reasons I can't articulate, but understand to have caused my constant denial. On some level, I knew Antony would end up in prison. But not for this. I assumed he'd be charged with murder; another moment of madness leading to his anger erupting so fiercely, so uncontrollably that he would hit somebody too hard, killing them. I never thought he'd be capable of hurting little girls. I always believed he had a natural affinity with younger children and animals. But that's how abusers cover their tracks isn't it?

Antony was grooming me, just as he'd done with those poor women all those years go. He'd enlisted his own mother as his accomplice by keeping her quiet with a simple smile, his eyes cast on the floor.

Only now I can see that his demeanor was not one of mental handicap, but of guilt.

DI SILVER

'They're releasing him without charge.'

The words send a reverberation across the office, like sound waves from one of those electric guitars one of the members of Antony's band *Blue Wave* used to play. Oh, I've heard of them alright, I've just never listened as intently to their lyrics as I did five minutes ago, searching for an unconscious connection to his black soul. Antony wrote *Schoolday Blues* when I was just a nipper, barely able to read or write.

'It's a love story about an older boy attracted to a younger girl.'

'It's irrelevant to the case unless you want to retrain as a barrister?'

'Ha ha, very funny.'

I notice the pile of paperwork flooding Locke's arms.

'What have you got there?'

'These are the files for the Wells case.'

'And why have you got them?'

'Because we're not going to need them in an hour.'

'Are you taking them down to the store room?'

'I'm considering it.'

I lower my voice and lean towards her. 'What are you up to?'

'I think Sophie's murder might be linked to the knife-wielding rapist.'

'Same knife?'

'Identical.'

I nod my head and catch a glimpse of the Chief over her shoulder.

'Scarper. I'll get him onside.'

As Locke skirts the corner, almost knocking the money plant Dawson has now decided to litter the office with onto the floor, I catch DCI Black with a wave of my hand as Locke disappears down the corridor, through the double doors, and into the evidence room.

'How can I help you?'

'I was wondering if you were pursuing a case against Isla for wasting police time?'

'The Super doesn't think it wise.'

'That's not like Dawson.'

'He said it would portray the force as resourceless and incompetent.'

'I agree, it's probably best to ignore the whole debacle and pray the media find something else to cling onto.'

'I think they already have,' he nods towards the window overlooking the city street, directing my attention to the circus of reporters stood in front of the entrance.

'They want blood.'

'Whose?'

'Whoever they can blame for releasing Wells without charge.'

'Aren't they miles out of their way?'

'Some of them are swarming Ashfield as we speak.'

'Vultures.'

KATE

It's stuffy and I'm beginning to feel claustrophobic, but I don't complain about the heat or the lack of oxygen inside the car. I open my window and breathe in the heady scent of rosemary and lavender from the front garden, mixing with Steven's musky aftershave, leaving a sickly taste in the back of my throat. We sit in silence, listening to the distant hum of traffic from the A-road at the back of the house and the gentle birdsong above while unsaid words begin to swell between us.

'I'm sorry.'

I glance at him as he stares out of the windscreen at the road ahead.

'You've got nothing to be sorry about. I should have been there for you. I wish I was. Am I really that difficult to talk to?'

I place my hand on his forearm. 'No.'

This has nothing to do with you.

'I didn't want it to change things between us. I was afraid you'd look at me differently.'

'But you're not to blame.'

'That's not what I mean. I didn't want you to think of me in that way.'

Weak. Vulnerable.

'You're one of the strongest women I know.'

He always used to joke about his mother's inner

strength, so I guess he means we're both even on that score. That'll be a first.

'I don't want you to feel sorry for me or to feel as though you've got to walk on eggshells. I'm not made of glass. I've survived the worst.'

'You don't have to be strong either.'

He grips my hand, entwining his fingers between mine.

'I know you can take care of yourself, but we all need someone to hold us once in a while. I'm glad you told me.'

I squeeze his hand, forcing myself to smile.

'That's my girl.'

I try not to show my discomfort at his choice of words. I'm nobody's *girl*.

The memories that linger at the back of my mind waiting for the opportunity to impede on my life are no longer crouched in the corners but are scurrying about, growing larger, threatening to jump out at me. Triggered by a flash of scent or the texture of a piece of clothing. Sometimes a sound or thought causes sparks of broken images to flit across my vision. But, as I sit here, they take on a physiological power. Steven doesn't notice me flinch as a piece of hair falls loose from the scrunchie holding it in place, dancing across the back of my neck like fingertips stroking my skin. The heavy ache in the pit of my stomach forcing me forwards as his denim-clad thigh grazes my leg.

These are the things I can't tell Steven because to do so means to admit that I was once not able to say no. That I was once a naive fourteen-year-old girl with sexual impulses. That instead of looking forward to taking my exams and leaving school to begin a career in health and social care, I was living two separate lives. In one of them, I was an innocent school girl. And in the other I was a young woman on the verge of a breakdown, struggling to conform to the rules of adulthood whilst in a relationship with an adult six years too old for me.

Having to keep my two selves apart was difficult at first, but it became easier when I lost touch with my friends and fell out with my parents. When you're in a situation it's hard to see things objectively. But now, twenty-eight years later, after a two-year long relationship with a paedophile, I've had the time to reconfigure events. The ones I remember, at least.

Though I'm more inclined to fear myself these days than that vile specimen of a human being, I'm afraid of what might happen if I came face-to-face with Antony.

The street lights cast an orange glow over the car crawling to a stop on the verge of the wet pavement. I step away from the window, hoping they haven't seen me and stand rooted to the spot, not daring to move in case my shadow alerts them to the fact I am home.

I glance back to see Steven making his way to the door, his eyes fixed on me, promising silently to lie to them for me.

It's been like this for days. Keeping up the pretence I've gone away to visit relatives, when in fact, I can't bear to look anyone in the eye. The thought of leaving the house frightens me more each time they come with unwavering dedication and set features.

Steven returns upstairs and closes the door of the bedroom. Hemmed in, unable to exit as I please, I'm forced to repeat what I've already told him.

'I'm not ready.'

'This isn't going to go away.'

'I can't face it.'

'You don't have to do this alone. I'll be right beside you. You don't even have to speak.'

I don't trust myself not to.

My mobile phone vibrates, moving slowly towards the edge of the bedside table.

I stare at it, willing it to stop. Another missed call from DI Locke. Another missed opportunity to put all of this right again. To get justice for what happened to me.

But my head is stuck in the past. Nightmares. Flashbacks. It's all coming back. I keep being awoken from another vision feeling just as unsafe in the present as I did back then in my schoolgirl dress, forced to remove my knickers before I could leave Antony's grimy bedroom.

Waves of panic rise up to my chest, constricting my breath which comes in shallow gulps as I try to force the memories back as I used to. But now that I've opened the box they've taken on a power of their own.

'Kate, this is hurting you more than you realise. You have to undo this chain he has over you.'

'I don't have to do anything!'

The voice doesn't sound like my own. I steady myself, flattening my hands on the bedside cabinet as my phone begins to vibrate again.

'Leave it,' I say, too late.

He answers, dropping the phone into my hand. With

no choice, I press the phone to my ear.

'Yes?'

'Mum?'

'Lisa, love, how are you?' I manage to say through trembling lips.

'Mum, what's going on? Dad said you'd gone away, but . . . he's acting weird.'

'Everything's fine.'

'I've been trying to get hold of you but you're not answering your phone. I'd started to think he'd done you in and buried you under the patio,' she laughs nervously.

'Mum?'

'Really, I'm fine. Your dad's being melodramatic as usual. Why don't we meet for coffee next week? I've got a few days off.'

'Yeah, sure. Look, I don't know what's going on, but-'

'I've got to go, darling. We'll speak soon.'

I glare at Steven before slamming the phone down onto the cabinet.

'You should have told her.'

'And say what?'

'She deserves to know.'

'I can't.'

He turns and leaves the room, shaking his head.

I have no intention of marking my daughter's memories of me; her strong, capable, loving mother subjected to *that*.

I return to the living room and set about wiping down the furniture with an unsteady hand clenching the polishing wipe a little too tight. The mirror reflects back the image of a ghost I once thought I knew, who now resembles a shell harbouring discord and frustration.

'Why won't anyone leave me alone?' I whisper into the dimly lit bedroom.

I glance around the empty room. Needing to clear my head, I make my way into the bathroom to cleanse the dirt I feel settling on my skin from Steven's unwavering gaze.

'It doesn't have to be this way,' a voice from within reassures me. 'There is a way out.'

'Don't I know it.'

I jump, realising Steven has made his way towards the top of the staircase, yawning, ready to glide into bed.

'Who are you talking to?'

'Nobody.'

'You're a strange one tonight,' he says, ruffling my hair in that childish way he does when he intends to use banter to draw me away from self-induced misery. But it won't work this time. I'm far too gone.

'I'll see you in bed?'

His question hangs in the air. I mumble 'sure', closing the bathroom door behind me.

After a hot shower, I continue downstairs and head for the kitchen, hoping to relieve the cloggy atmosphere with more polishing. Once I'm sufficiently tired enough I head upstairs for bed.

The cuckoo clock chimes 2:00am. I've lost two hours again.

Settling beneath the duvet covers, I turn to face the wall, listening to the sound of Steven's rhythmic snoring, willing sleep to find me.

TERESA

I was clearing out his room when I found it. Antony had finally left home to make his own way in the world. Amongst his things were the usual: clothes, the empty rucksack he took to school, a few boxed figurines of superheroes that Christopher had bought him hoping they might be worth some money a few years down the line, and a couple of CDs. If it weren't for the fact that I'd found Antony's journal stuffed down the side of his mattress I might not have known that he blamed me for abandoning him. All of the pages inside it were left blank except for one entry, dated Friday 15th July 1982.

Mum's sending me to boarding school.

When I first saw those words all those years ago I thought he was punishing me, having left the diary open on his bedside table, hoping I'd see it. Perhaps he thought by finding it I'd let him stay. But it's odd that the only entry he made coincided with the pinnacle date I'd given up trying to fix him. I thought that sending him off to a residential school would help him learn the value of friendships, teach him right from wrong in a way that I clearly hadn't pressed upon him hard enough. I thought he'd develop his independence. I thought that if he left home he'd mature into a sensible, thoughtful man. I thought I was doing the right thing. How was I supposed to know that he would blame me for the things that happened there?

'The teacher who stole his childhood is no better or worse than Antony who went on to do the same thing,' Steven said. Maybe he's right.

After waving Antony off that Summer, I met Caroline during a shopping trip to BHS. We shared a bond so unlike the one I felt with Christopher. She understood me. Not just as a person, but as a woman, with needs. But, if I were to pinpoint the one defining moment that changed Antony from the misunderstood boy with learning difficulties to the angry, hostile man he became it would not be the moment I decided to send him off in his new uniform to St. Matthews. It would be the day he returned home to discover his mother sat across the table from Caroline, laughing, holding hands like old friends.

Did he sense the longing in my eyes as I gazed into hers?

It was Caroline who caught the look of confusion on his face. She told me later that as I sat there oblivious to him entering the room that he stared at me as though I was a stranger. I turned from the look of horror etched onto Caroline's face to see my son hiss at her before marching from the kitchen and stomping up the stairs.

'Why didn't you tell me he was there?'

'It will do him good to know now, won't it?'

'No, it won't. I'll go upstairs and see if he's alright.'

'Don't you think you deserve to be happy too? Christopher has his wife.'

'It's always been just us.'

'You think having me around is going to change that?'

I narrowed my eyes at her comment.

'He has problems processing emotions.'

'He seems perfectly acute in that department.'

'He's my son. No matter how much I love you his needs come first.'

'Even at the detriment of your own happiness?'

'Sacrifice is a part of parenting, Caroline.'

Of course, she'd have known that if her children still lived with her.

I went upstairs to find his bedroom door locked. When he didn't answer I began hammering on the door. When he failed to respond I kicked it, full pelt. Then, realising losing my temper wasn't going to solve the rift that had fallen between us, I pleaded for him to come out and talk to me. That's when heavy metal rock music began to blast from the stereo Christopher had bought him before he left for boarding school.

'Turn it down!'

There was no answer.

I called up to him from the stairs. 'Fine. Have it your way. Do what you want. I don't care anymore.'

'Leaving him to stew?'

I smiled weakly.

I eyed the tea and toast cluttering the dining table.

'Peace offering.'

'I accept.'

We were about to retreat to bed when Antony appeared in the doorway.

'You haven't eaten since you got home.'

'This isn't my home.'

'No?'

'I don't live here.'

'For the next six weeks, you do.'

'While you're home for the Summer holidays, your mother expects you to eat with us at the table.'

'Who's us?'

Caroline holds out her hand, but Antony sniffs. 'I'm your mother's friend.'

He turns to me. 'I didn't think you had any.'

'We've known each other a while.'

'You must think I'm stupid.'

'I'm sorry, I didn't know I had to seek your approval as to who I spend my time with.'

'You're replacing me with that . . . lesbian.'

I had no idea how to reply. I was trying to move on with my life, find someone to talk to, spend time with, but replace him? Never.

'You're jealous of a woman?'

'I can't compete. Neither can dad.'

'Your father isn't-'

'I know. I know. Save it,' he said, grabbing some orange juice from the fridge, glugging it down without stopping.

'In this house we use glasses.'

'In this house, my mum's decided to start shagging women while I'm stuck in that hell hole prison.'

'I sent you to *school* for a better education. Don't you enjoy it there?'

'What do you think?'

The truth was I'd never thought to ask.

'You have no idea what it's like. You're too consumed with your own happiness now you've got rid of me.'

'If it's so bad there why didn't you write to me?'

'You really are stupid aren't you?'

'Don't talk to your mother like that.'

'My mother?'

'You ungrateful little shit-'

'Speak to your mother with more respect.'

'Respect?'

'I've fed you, clothed you, stuck up for you, and you repay me by insulting my intelligence and choice of lover.'

'Lovers?' he laughs.

'Go to your room. I don't want to fucking see you.'

He came towards me and Caroline baulked. I could smell the venom on his breath.

'They vet everything sent in or out of the school.'

I stepped back into the counter top.

'I didn't know. You never told me.'

'They won't let me write to you. They said I'll get homesick.'

'If you're not happy there . . .'

'Really, I can come home. Why didn't you say?'

A mix of anger and shame burned through my skull.

Caroline came between us, placing her hand on my shoulder. The moment we touched a spark of heat rose up his cheeks and Antony bolted from the room.

That's when the phone rang.

'He's done what?'

I heard her the first time but I couldn't assemble the words in my throbbing head.

I dropped the receiver and it bounced off the counter top and smacked the tiled floor. Caroline escorted me into the living room, where I fell into an armchair and sat staring into space.

Kneeling at my feet she looked up at me. 'What is it,

what's wrong?'

'Antony isn't going back after the Summer holidays.'

The disdain of my comment was obvious.

'He set fire to his teacher's bedroom.'

'You mean he tried to kill him?'

'They're treating it as arson. They've suspended him indefinitely.'

She rubbed my shoulder as though willing her strength to soak through me. 'Teresa, I'm so sorry.'

Antony flung the door open and stood over us. 'The lovers are at it again.'

'She birthed you,' said Caroline through thin lips.

How could I defend him? He'd brought trouble to my door, and all that bothered him was my choice of partner.

He pursed his lips and made a mock kissing noise.

Caroline jumped up and went to slap him across his smug face, but I caught her hand before she made the impact.

'You're a bitch. Dad was right.'

'Your father had an affair!'

'You probably bored him to death.'

'Maybe he couldn't stand the sight of you.'

'I'm going upstairs. Try and keep the noise down, yeah?'

Caroline barged past me, clutching the lower hem of Antony's shirt in her fist.

'Leave him, Caroline.'

'I'm not going to let him talk to you like that.'

'Don't worry, he'll cool down. He just needs some space.'

I had no intention of telling Caroline that tonight would be his last in my house. I wanted him gone.

The following morning, I stood at the door. 'I'll be here if you need me.'

In one hand he held his old school rucksack, the one I later learned he'd filled with gas canisters which he used to light Mr Thatcher's bedroom up with, mistaking it for his study. I didn't want to acknowledge that my son had not only become a man in that boarding school but had also become a stranger. In his other hand he held a box.

Christopher honked the horn, waiting for Antony to hurry up and get inside the Cortina. He offered no assistance as I attempted to hoist the box into the boot. He stood beside me, one hand on the bumper, kneeling down to tie his shoelace. He looked up to me, lowered his voice and said, 'you couldn't have prevented it.'

I suppose he was right. The damage had been done. Antony's fall from grace was inevitable really, wasn't it?

DI SILVER

This has got to be one of the hardest conversations I'm about to have in my fifteen-year career with the force. Notifying someone of a death would have been preferable.

Locke sits beside me, chewing gum, making an irritating snapping sound as she attempts to crack it like a whip against her teeth.

I pull the car up alongside Kate's house. The grass that only a few weeks ago had been cut back, green, is now overgrown and yellowing. The mud surrounding the long tufts is cracked. Recycling is piled high in several boxes, some of the glass bottles protruding through the cardboard. Tin cans scattered across the ground.

I follow Locke from the car towards the front door. She glances through the window then back to the rubbish left on the ground to one side of the house.

'She must have had a cleaning splurge.'

What she means is *at least the mess is outside*.

I lift the letterbox and slam it down harder than intended.

Locke gives me a daggered look.

'It's the wind.'

She rolls her eyes.

Kate opens the door, her complexion pallid. 'I heard.'

'You saw the news?'

She shakes her head. 'Radio.' Looking from me to Locke she steps aside. 'You'd better come in.'

KATE

This morning I recounted more of the two years of my trauma to Steven, leaving the gory details out. I think he sees me less of a victim and more of a survivor now. 'I can't believe you went through all that alone' and 'you're amazing' are his most used phrases for what he says "I've been through."

I'm on my way out the door when I spot the gleaming white Audi. DI Locke approaches me first, as always, her gaze warm. DI silver stands back with one hand in the pocket of his neatly pressed trousers.

'I guess you want to come in?'

They follow me inside without uttering a word and I take a deep breath before leading them into the kitchen. The kettle is still hot from the coffee I've just made so I absentmindedly pour water into two cups, remembering DI Locke takes her coffee black.

'Thanks,' she says, taking a sip of the oily looking liquid that makes me want to heave.

DI Silver coughs as I pull out a chair to offer him a seat, but through the tense atmosphere, I can tell they'd rather not make themselves comfortable.

'You know Antony was released,' she says, holding my gaze.

'Doesn't everyone know?' I stutter.

'The CPS thought it was in the public's interest not to

pursue the charges, under the circumstances.'

'What circumstances?'

'The original claimant was murdered.'

'I heard. You think it's got something to do with the trial?'

'It's highly likely.'

'What now?'

'My colleague and I were hoping to ask you a few more questions. You're not obliged to answer, but it may help us with something else.'

'Right.'

DI Silver straightens up and I watch as he takes a sip of his boiling hot tea.

'Add another drop of milk if you like.'

He turns towards the fridge and pours a dollop of milk into his cup.

'Biscuits?'

'Please.'

'How are you feeling?' says DI Locke, dipping a HobNob into her tea.

Brutally assessing my current emotions, 'like shit.'

She offers me a tight smile.

There's no need for pretence, not since they found me comatose on the doorstep with a bottle of vodka wedged between my thighs at 8:00pm one evening last week. That, of course, was during my supposed "relative visiting holiday." They've seen the worst of me so we're a little more honest with one another now.

'No biscuits for you, Detective?' I motion to DI Silver.

He pats his stomach. 'Diet.'

I sit at the dining table in front of DI Locke, waiting

for DI Silver to take his usual seat at the end of the table with a copy of last Sunday's newspaper open in front of him.

'Why do you do this?' I ask, genuinely intrigued.

'To get the bad guys off the street.'

'But that's not right is it, because most of them get away with it.'

I know what she wants to say 'you shouldn't think like that' but she doesn't. She can't. She has to remain professional.

'It's our job to hand over the evidence, the CPS to prosecute, and the defence to contradict them.'

'You couldn't guarantee a conviction.'

'No, but the media will eat him alive now he's walked away from this.'

She's right. Antony's life, as he once knew it is now well and truly over. Which is no less than he deserves.

'Have you thought any more about what I said the last time we spoke?'

She means therapy, paid for by the government for other souls who happen to have found themselves in the unfortunate situation of being part of a historic sex abuse case years after they thought their ordeal was over.

'I can give you the number of someone highly experienced in trauma.'

'I'm fine.'

If you picked me up and shook me I'd rattle from the amount of Valium and codeine I've been using to hold myself together.

She offers me a knowing look but chooses not to voice her concern. I can see it in her eyes. She's worried about me. They all are. Even Doctor Lambeth, who has discontinued my medication, asking to meet with me to "discuss treatment options" forcing me to self-medicate. 'Only rely on yourself' my dad always said, and he was right, wasn't he?

Steven was an emotional wreck this morning when we heard that Antony had been released with only a suspended sentence for obtaining indecent images of children, and thanks to my own decision, long ago, to avoid personal contact with friends and family, I've nobody else to turn to.

Who wouldn't sneak pills into the bathroom, swallowing them down with a travel sized bottle of vodka to help them sleep with what I have latched onto my shoulders?

'You said you wanted to ask me something?'

'We'd like to clarify something you said during your informal interview.'

'Okay.'

'You said that you had been raped and that Antony came into the room to comfort you afterwards.'

'That's right. He did.'

'He came into the room, not back into the room?'

'Yes, that's what I said.'

'Kate, how often did Antony rape you?'

'What kind of fucked up question is that?'

'I understand this is difficult for you.'

'No, you don't. You haven't got the faintest idea what I've been through.'

'Okay, I can see how distressing this is for you.'

'Get out.'

DI Locke stands.

'Is that why my *non-statement* was deemed too

flimsy?'

'We had a strong case.'

'So why are you asking me all these questions, making me relive those years when you already know what happened?'

'It was just a hunch, that's all.'

DI Silver follows his colleague out of the living room, turns back to me and says, 'thank you for your time.'

I mumble a curt reply.

I'm glad to see the back of them when they close the front door, heading out into the wind so I can retreat back to my existence. And it is merely breathing I do now, unable to live as I once had in case the media pick up on my false unhappiness and decide to run with it. I feel like I can't even smile if I want to- as if I don't deserve to.

I stand at the window watching the detectives drive away. Realising the time I panic and grab my coat. The boss has already mentioned the bags beneath my eyes and my snappy temperament. I don't want him thinking I can't cope. What he doesn't know is that it's quelled only by stealing medication from my patients.

I return home from work around 5:00pm, shovelling carrier bags onto the counter top after a day filled with bathing, dressing, preparing food, and handing out medication to my clients. I stack the food away and head upstairs to lie down, unwanted thoughts undulating through my skull the moment I do.

'Not now.' I don't want to remember.

I rifle through my knick-knack drawer in the bedside cabinet and unfold the small slip of paper containing two blue pills. I place the 10mg Valium on my tongue and dart into the bathroom to scoop ice cold water into my mouth to wash them down with. Woozy and disorientated I don't question whether or not it's a good idea to drive to the local Co-Op in search of a small bottle of cherry brandy for a night-cap. I just do it.

I spend the evening curled up on the sofa whilst Steven rallies around me like a worried parent over a sick child. Dylan called to see how I was, but Steven couldn't get hold of Lisa. I'm glad really because she'd only start asking questions that I don't feel ready to explain away.

I retreat to bed early.

'I'll bring you up a hot chocolate.'

'I don't want anything. Honestly Steven, I'm okay.'

He shakes his head.

'I don't know what to do.'

I yawn, feigning tiredness. He switches off the light thinking I'm going to sleep.

Left alone in the dark, my eyes refusing to close I lie helpless as the shadows in the room elongate. The familiar sensation of being watched forces me to pull the covers up over my head.

In my mind, Antony stands beside the door staring at me. I shake uncontrollably beneath the duvet, covering my eyes with my hands to block out the flashing images that fight to grab my attention.

TERESA

Our lives are being dismantled by the media. Despite Rachel's promise to write exclusive, the reporters still hover outside, awaiting permission to come to the door and speak to me.

I haven't spoken to Antony since the trial collapsed. Perhaps he's too consumed with anxiety to worry about his mother.

The weekend brings sunshine and I spend much of it outdoors turning over weeds and replanting the crocuses alongside snowdrops that trail along the wall of the house, giving the impression that the garden is much longer than it is. Their lilac trimmed heads look beautiful alongside the pearl white snowdrops, flanked on either side by blush pink cyclamen which grows in clumps beneath the fickle hawthorn bush.

I take the tools of my trade and step inside the potting shed, steering around a bag of soil left haphazardly on the floor in front of a spade. I trip and fall awkwardly on my side. I escape the garden in a fit of annoyance to wash my hands in the kitchen sink before leaving to top up the petrol in the VW Golf. By the time I hit the road my mind is frazzled.

I wasn't thinking as I drove along the terraced lined streets searching for somewhere to stop so I didn't acquire another parking ticket. The streets had recently been laid with grit and signs declared *NO PARKING THURSDAY AND FRIDAY*. I didn't notice the Toyota Rav 4 until I hit it.

My pride is bruised more than the front bumper of my car. I blame Antony, the case, the constant struggle as I delve into the past searching for the cause of my son's actions.

DI SILVER

'That's it then?'

'Suppose so.'

'Seems unjust, doesn't it?'

I know what Locke means. Four months of investigating, compiling evidence to forward onto the CPS, arresting, and then interviewing Antony as well as band members, family members, friends, work colleagues and, acquaintances- now he walks free.

A tech guy discovered the 1,400 indecent downloaded images of children on his phone purely by accident whilst looking into another case. The IP address for a known paedophile in-directly linked us to Wells.

Locke angles the screen to give me a better view of the CCTV footage which took over a week to have sent over due to the many atrocities of paperwork we had to break through in order to force the council to release it.

The image is grainy, probably caused by grime on the lens. The woman's figure appears distorted. If I didn't know better I might have suggested we were looking at a man, but her clumsy gait and the brief glimpse of a fur-trim boot peeping from the hem of a long out-of-date, over-sized coat, suggests that Sophie's late night caller was a female.

Locke pauses, zooms in, and attempts to mark areas of the screenshot. 'The image is so poor I can't capture a definitive height or weight.'

'We're looking for a female.'

'Isla?'

'I doubt she'd want to damage her own case. Besides, she's too tall.'

Locke runs her finger across the glass. 'You're right. We're looking for someone large built, short,' squinting, 'and dark-haired.'

'Wells' daughter?'

'How would she know where to find Sophie unless she knew what her father had done to the girl?'

'The internet. And, let's not make assumptions.'

Locke turns to face me. 'She's already smacked a reporter in the mouth.'

'Her police record did show a prior assault charge.'

'Let's bring her in.'

KATE

After the detectives visit on Friday, I've spent most of the weekend in a state of perpetual unease. Going through the motions without taking anything in. Even the dinner we were invited to by friends of Steven, went by without retention. I just can't seem to see past the bubble wrap I've wound around myself.

Ian Banks, the Crown Prosecution Advocate called me this morning as I was making my way into work to personally thank me for my time and to wish me well. Antony never made it to the introductory session and now the court are calling me to "wish me well." Bollocks to them all.

I force myself to focus on the task at hand, pushing all thoughts of the non-starting case aside.

I've managed to convince Ms Smythes to have a wash and take her medication, but I've noticed the spark in her eyes has left her.

'How are you doing?'

'Not too good love,' she says, taking another biscuit from the plate in front of her and dipping it into her tea.

'Is there anything I can do?'

'No, love,' she sighs.

A beat of silence follows before she tells me that today is the anniversary of her son's death.

'He was three. Got hit by a car on the corner of the

road. The sod didn't stop and when they rushed him into Frenchay, he'd already passed away.'

'That's awful. I'm so sorry.'

'Nout anyone could do.'

'And it's today?'

She nods her head grimly. 'He'd be fifty-seven next week.'

'I can't imagine the pain you must have gone through, are still going through.'

'Everyone on the street came round on his birthday to celebrate. In those days, people stood by one another. Everyone's moved on now or died.'

It's sad to think that her memories might have been lost in the minds of others.

'Mr Hitchote, across the road, he remembers. He'll still bring over a slice of cake and a card on Thursday. Silly cow, ain't I?'

'No. I think it's important to remember our loved ones.'

'I struggle sometimes. It's lonely being old,' she laughs. But I don't find it funny.

As I was growing up, children played outside, the front door was always left on the latch and nobody saw anything wrong with it. How naive we were to believe that nothing could happen to us, that nothing could touch us.

I twist awkwardly in my seat, brushing away invisible cobwebs as the memory of hands pawing at my skin linger like ghostly fingers.

'I don't like to leave you, but I have to go. I've got another call to make before lunch.'

'Thanks love. I value your time. I don't know what I'd

do without my girls.'

'You don't ever have to feel alone. There's always someone willing to spend time with you.'

I make my way out of the living room towards the door and turn back to Ms Smythes.

She smiles weakly and waves.

I know how hard it is to paint a fake smile on your face when really, you feel broken.

As I near the door I turn back to her. 'I appreciate the time we spend together. I don't do this for the money.'

'I can tell.'

As I turn the key in the ignition I can't help wondering if she was trying to tell me something. Between the words we use is a silent voice, waiting to be heard.

I'm in half a mind to walk over to Mr Hitchcote's and ask him to pay her a visit when my phone rings; a warning not to interfere in others business, to grow too emotionally attached to my clients.

Loud white noise greets me as I accept the call.

'Hello?'

'Hey.'

'Steven?'

The wind and the hum of traffic carry over his voice as if he's speaking through water.

'. . . can't hear you.'

'I'll call you back. The line's rubbish.'

It's not until I slip the phone back into my pocket that I realise the sound wasn't coming from the phone at all, but from my head. I glance up and down the busy street, noting the swarms of people traveling from work back to their families, continuing on with their lives. Unlike mine, that I feel has stalled, leaving me feeling empty and confused.

My arm burns. I look down to where I've been rubbing the skin raw with my nail. Small dots of blood speckle the surface so I dig deeper until I feel the wonderful rush of pain.

I must fight to stay on top of things. I must stop my mind from wandering back to the past. I'm frightened of what might happen if I don't.

TERESA

When I receive the call from Jacky, I'm about to put the shopping away. I was awoken by the letterbox flapping shut several times to be met with a pile of newspapers peppering the ground, Antony's face plastered all over the front pages, reworded lines of text he's supposed to have said printed below; false stories those lying two-faced women used to destroy my son. The media haven't yet tired of their long slog through the murky waters of Antony's life.

Jacky sounds agitated and out of breath.

'Hannah's been arrested.'

'What for?'

'Those detectives who keep sniffing about said they saw her leaving that house. You know the one where that woman lived who made all those claims.'

'Sophie?'

'That's 'er.'

'But, why would Hannah be there?'

'I dunno.'

'Do they think she killed her?'

'They're barking up the wrong tree, ain't they. So you comin' over 'ere or what?'

'Of course. I'll be with you in fifteen minutes.'

I haven't seen Jacky since Antony was placed in police custody, after the bail hearing. I still haven't heard from Antony either, but I've begun to suspect it might have something to do with all those assessments and reports the psychologist forced on him. I'll bet you anything they tried to make out I was a terrible mother. He ignored my calls, cancelled my visiting order, and as he's above the age of eighteen I had no permission to speak with his defence barrister once she took him on as a client. Why he paid her after her shocking lack of action I'll never know. Since his release Isla's exclusive has been revoked due to her promiscuity, paid sex work, and a history of dishonesty. She made a similar claim against a man five years ago, a case that was also thrown out of court.

As I hurry down the stairs, I start to remember things from the last couple of weeks. Stupid things really. Like the way I bit my lip and slipped through security for courtroom number two during Antony's bail hearing.

The court smelt of varnish and wax. The air conditioning forced the hairs on my arms to stand on end, then later the same response to the words they used to describe my son: a sexual predator. The sense of immediacy. The dirty looks I received whilst entering the room. The nosy locals who sat in the public gallery on faux wood seats that resembled those you might find in a church. The eagle-eyed journalists sat pens in hand, notebooks at the ready, preparing to enlighten the evening newspapers with their version of that morning's events. Antony boxed in like a caged animal behind bullet-proof glass.

Jennifer Tate, Antony's defence barrister sat opposite me as QC Weatherby left her chambers to stride through the court, her shoes slapping the floor before taking to her bench. The determined air she wove through the grand room, sat straight with a tidy bun placed high on her head, dark haired, and brown eyed she looked plain for a judge.

Everyone was seated except for the Crown Advocate who stood on thin legs hidden behind an immaculate grey lined suit awaiting his chance to present the court with the so-called evidence. That was the part I'd been most frightened of. Nobody had told me what concrete pillars they had ready to stack against my boy.

Mr Monroe was a thin, balding man who collected several pieces of paper from the small desk in front of him and proceeded towards the stand. The clerk swore him in. Mr Monroe took a sip of water from a styrofoam cup before he spoke.

The Crown Prosecution Advocate phrased the case as 'difficult and tragic.' At the time I found his words too sordid to comprehend so zoned out, picking at one of my newly applied faux nails until we were called to leave.

Why am I thinking of this now?

Oh, yes. She was there.

Hannah.

She sat alone.

Why wasn't Jacky there to support her husband?

DI SILVER

The call came in an hour ago. The woman sounded desperate, inconsolable, her words a jumbled mess.

I followed Locke to the house and now I stand over the body.

The pathologist, Dr. Chloe Bridges, looks up at me, tilting her head to one side and confirms my suspicions.

'Broken neck. Ligature marks. Strong likelihood that it was suicide, but under the circumstances, I'd like to perform further examination on the body.'

The Wells case has resulted in two deaths so far. And this one can't have been caused by Sophie's suspected killer. Hannah was being interviewed, and after twenty-four hours has been released without charge due to a lack of forensic evidence. We're still looking into several lines of inquiry.

'Come on,' says Locke, slipping her arm through mine. 'We've got work to do.'

I feel the corpses eyes on the back of my neck as though even in death the final image they saw cannot be erased.

The purple neck, the bruises, the bloodshot eyes, the bitten tongue, all point to suicide, but why do I get the feeling someone else was here?

'Come on Paul, we've got a house call to make,' she says, dragging me away.

I follow Locke towards the car, my eyes on Chloe, lifting the body up onto a stretcher and wheeling it over to the private ambulance.

KATE

I've been awake since 5:00am, watching the sun rise up through the slats in the blind. The doorbell rings unexpectedly around midday just as I'm getting dressed.

I know as soon as I pull the door open to reveal DI Locke and DI Silver that the reason for their visit can't be a good one. Their morose greetings deliver a magnetic pull to flee that sends adrenaline coursing through my veins. As they invite themselves to sit on the sofa, I tidy away empty cups of long-cold tea trying to ignore the ripples of dread that send pain shooting down my arms. I drop a teaspoon on the floor, collect it up, and dart into the kitchen to wipe the beads of sweat springing to my forehead with the sleeve of my sweater.

I sit uncomfortably beside them and twist a thread of hair between thumb and forefinger, as I always do when nervous. A habit I don't remember starting, but know may lead to later hair-pulling when alone.

DI Locke, speaks first. I glance at the floor as she reveals the shocking news.

Tears fall free down my cheeks as I clamp my lips together to stop myself from screaming.

'Dead?' I say, through gritted teeth and pursed lips.

'We thought it would be better if you heard it from us.'

'How did he die?'

'It looks like suicide.'

While I was contemplating how to tell my children - with Steven's advice - that I'd been repeatedly raped as a child, Antony had been making a noose to hang himself with.

'Did he confess?'

'Come clean you mean?'

'Most people leave a note.'

'As far as I'm aware, he did not.'

'So he gets away with it.'

I stand to give the detectives signal to leave, but DI Silver remains seated.

'There is the option of a civil lawsuit, for damages.'

'I've no intention of taking the man's inheritance.'

'It would be criminal injury compensation from the state as a result of your psychological distress, a consequence of his death . . .'

DI Locke offers her partner a forceful look, demonstrating the tenderness of their companionship.

'I assure you I will not be taking legal action against a dead man. He can rot in hell for all I care.'

I almost wince, the words leaving a sour taste in my mouth.

It wasn't his fault. I've come to realise that now. He had problems. It was in the papers. A limited capacity to understand emotions, social cues, a cognitive delay. It doesn't make what he did right, but it does explain things.

I shiver from the involuntary memory of his denim-clad leg scraping against my thigh as he held me, sobbing into his chest, after the first rape. He had no idea why I was upset. The fuckwit.

DI Locke blinks slowly as if siding with me. If I knew her under different circumstances we might have become friends, but as it happens her presence in my home, bringing with her once more news that I'd rather had been kept from me, sets my head on fire.

'Excuse me, but I have a migraine coming on, do you mind?'

Getting the hint this time before I blow up and tell them to leave, both detectives walk away from the house without so much as a backward glance. I sink down onto the floor with the thick UPVC door behind me, feeling the draft on my buttocks drift up to where my hands sit shaking on bony knees.

Antony must have panicked, committing suicide to end the embarrassment of a public trial by the media.

'Stupid man.'

But he had the right idea.

Is there a better way of ensuring your reputation remains intact than by claiming innocence through killing yourself?

If I had my way, he'd remain locked up behind bars until he died of pneumonia in his cold, nine by six foot cell.

I think of his mother then. He must have one. At least I presume she's still alive. A wife. Perhaps even children of his own. My stomach tightens in knots of dread then, thinking he might have offered them the same comfort he did me. Being held after the trauma is almost worse than the abuse itself.

I walk without purpose towards the front door, breathe in the fresh scent of August rain and step out onto the stone path. My legs feel as though they're going to buckle beneath me.

I glance up at the sky and wonder what God would allow someone capable of such cruelty to escape conviction whilst I'm forced to remain imprisoned by the memories that cut me off from everything I once believed bore safety and opportunity. My eyes trace the sullied streets, grimy pavements, slick with rain where anyone, even men like him can tread.

What I would do to taste the freedom that comes from leaving it all behind. Just as I had intended the day I walked out of my childhood home never to look back to see the forlorn face of my father and the hardened gaze of my mother who knew nothing of the dangers their daughter had faced. An image of my fourteen-year-old self comes to me then, curled in a ball beneath the duvet, crying silently into her pillow, willing the lord to snatch her from sleep and welcome her into the arms of death. Wondering what happened to my parents is not something I should be concerning myself with now.

Guilt is a killer.

I blink back tears and allow the rain to cascade down the collar of my sweater and pool around my slippered feet, soaking through to my numbed skin. I reach out a shaking hand to open the gate, stepping onto the pavement tentatively. I don't glance behind me to see the front door swinging wildly back and forth in the wind as I make my way towards the car.

TERESA

Rachel appears at my side in an instant. Having taken off her navy blue jacket and hung it over the doorframe. I'm about to stir the coffee when the doorbell chimes. Excusing myself I leave her to find a seat in the living room. Before I've even opened the door I know by the way their shadows fall onto the concrete path, slick with rain, who they are and what they want. I'm in no mood to entertain their pleas for another sensational story.

I return to the living room annoyed and fidgety. I snap at Rachel as she places her bag down on the coffee table.

'I thought you said they'd bugger off now I've agreed to speak with you.'

'Oh, they will, eventually.'

'Well, I want them gone or you can kiss goodbye to your career.'

I don't think she realises how fully-charged I am. I could damage her, sue the arses off them all for killing my boy.

I've given her exclusive rights to anything concerning Antony's upbringing so long as her newspaper refrains from printing any lies disguised as evidence as revealed from outside sources. Unlike those other newspapers, *The Bristol Times* has stuck to their promise. But I'd still like the media circus outside my house to fuck off.

'If they knock again, I'll answer the door,' she says.

With that she sits back in the armchair as if she owns the place and pulls out her Dictaphone.

'How are you coping?'

She means how do I feel about my son's death.

'Numb.'

She nods her head in sympathy, but I get the impression that she's glad. They all are. Once you've been accused of something so horrific it takes more than murder to put it right.

'He didn't kill himself. Of that I'm certain. He was a weak-minded man, but he wouldn't have done that to me.'

'You think someone staged his death?' she says, leaning forwards.

'He didn't rape Sophie, you know.'

She doesn't agree with my verdict. I can see it in her eyes.

'Can I speak about the dead?'

'Sophie?'

'Yes.'

'Go on?'

'She told the police that Antony had lifted up her skirt and fondled her.'

Something I still find hard to believe, considering he knew nothing of sex aside from the fact that it created babies and had something to do with your lower regions.

'I heard that she'd invented it. The dates didn't stack up. Her family moved away?'

'They were Irish travellers. She fell pregnant just after her sixteenth birthday to a boy who'd proposed to marry her. He went to prison and her family moved away a week later. She fell into addiction with a gorger (one of us) and her daughter was taken into care.'

'I heard.'

'I just thought it might help to explain things. You see I think the media coverage exploited my son. It left him wide open to all sorts of claims. False ones.'

'I agree. It should have been handled better.'

I settle my eyes on Rachel Harper's long bare legs and small heeled court shoes as she waits for me to continue.

'They arrested him in front of his wife and daughter. Can you imagine . . .?'

She shakes her head.

'She was a state this morning.'

'Who?'

'Jacky. She found him.'

I snatch a breath to keep my voice steady. I don't want to break in front of her.

'There's something I can't get my head around though.'

'Go on?'

'Why did he commit suicide after walking free?'

'Shame?'

'He had nothing to be ashamed of. He didn't rape Sophie. Isla had signed an exclusive with the paper's before the CPS decided to take it to trial, and the other girl, the one who called in, refused to give a statement. They were lucky none of them were charged with perverting the course of justice.'

But none of that matters now. All I want to know is who assisted Antony's death. Who pushed him overboard and into the sea of suicidal intent?

I walk towards the window to allow a little air in and catch two lads - no older than Antony was when he got caught riding a stolen motorbike around the neighbourhood - running away from my car.

Bold bright blue letters run from bonnet to bumper along one side declaring that I am the *Paedo's Mum*.

DI SILVER

The Eastville knife-wielding rapist is behind bars. A tip-off from a prostitute in the early hours of this morning lead DI Blake and DI Flint to the man who had been spotted loitering on Fishponds Road, approaching hookers.

The girl, Jodie Mitchell, was approached by a man fitting the attacker's description around 1:00am. He'd told her he had a knife and asked if she liked it rough. She called the police when one of the working girls disappeared for ten minutes, thinking he'd got hold of her. The woman was found smacked out of her face in the park, but luckily her friend's drug-addled instincts were correct.

I don't do night shift work, but when Locke asks me if I'd go with her to speak to Jacky I oblige.

Antony's death has been treated as a suicide. Chloe is happy to release his body so the family can begin to arrange the funeral. It's a sad state of affairs that forces me to look at myself a little harder. What I see is a passionate, dedicated, loyal detective who wants to share what little free time he has with someone. Is that too much to ask for?

'Stop day-dreaming and hit the road,' says, Locke, smiling.

'Jacky will be pleased. She can finally lay her

husband to rest.'

'And the mother. I'm sure Teresa will be relieved too.'

KATE

I don't know how much time has passed but the sky is turning black as I make my way along the street towards the house.

I stand there, rooted to the very spot I stood in thirty years ago, full of hate and anger. Shame and guilt preventing me from telling anyone what had happened to me in there.

Antony comforted me afterwards. He came into the bedroom to undress and glanced up to see me shaking with fear, perched on the end of the bed.

I had a crush. A stupid childhood crush. But after a while, it began to feel like something close to love. It was a romance until the rape.

Before that, it was touching. A stray hand here, a gentle caress there. The cuddles soon became more forceful, more uncomfortable. It's clear to me now that Antony was oblivious. He had no idea that a hug was the last thing I wanted after what I'd just been forced to endure.

I felt weak. Hopeless. And stupid for believing it was anything more than abuse. As a child, I saw myself as streetwise. I was not one of those girls who ends up in a twisted relationship with the man who began grooming them the moment they grew breasts. But stood here now, on the pavement, looking up at the house, the downstairs lit with a single bulb, I realise what a fool I was for believing I could have prevented it. I was a child. A fourteen-year-old girl. It wasn't my fault. And on some level, I don't truly believe it was Antony's either.

TERESA

Hannah calls me in a panic just as Rachel is leaving. Her voice is muffled, but beneath her mumbled words I hear screaming. Not the kind of distressed screaming Jacky was making when she called to tell me my Antony was dead, but a kind of feral screaming you hear in a horror film.

'Nan, please come. She's gone mental.'

I slam the phone down and curse under my breath.

'Can't the woman get a bloody grip?'

I'm in two minds not to bother going over there, but collect the keys from my coat pocket and tear out of the door. The sky is dark and only one street lamp lights the way to my car. I start the engine and demist the windows.

I'm in no hurry to get there. Jacky has always been difficult to get along with. I suppose it helped that she was so obese and unhealthy that she rarely left the house. She spent most of her time on the laptop or on her phone, staring at pictures of what, I couldn't tell you, but it meant that even when I visited the house with her lying flat out on the sofa, I got to see Antony, alone.

JACKY

Hannah looks at me with disdain.

'There are two sides to every story, Hannah. The finger always gets pointed at the husband, the father, the son because it's easier that way.'

'You're saying Dad was accused because of his status?'

'Look what happened to Sophie. She realised her lie wouldn't stand up in court so she withdrew her statement, and that didn't get her far.'

'She was murdered, mum. That's nothing to smile about.'

I hadn't realised I was smiling.

'It was just a stupid schoolgirl fantasy that got out of hand, that's all.'

I reach down to where I've left a packet of Wotsits and cram a handful in my mouth.

'You can't minimise abuse, and it certainly wasn't a relationship. Sophie was underage,' says Hannah, matter-of-factly.

'She knew what she was doing.'

'How can you say that?'

'It came out that she was abused by her father. She wanted someone to pay and she decided to make an accusation. I don't think she knew how far it would go.'

'And the woman who said he raped her, she was lying

too?'

'She heard what Sophie was accusing him of and she ran with it to make money.'

'Why did my father hang himself?'

'I don't know.'

She looks at me then shakes her head.

'I'm saying it wasn't him, that's all.'

'You're saying dad was innocent?'

'Clever girl.'

I notice her tense at my blunt sarcasm.

'You knew he didn't do it and you didn't say anything when he was arrested. You let it almost go to trial. You let him go to prison.'

'He was on remand.'

'He was still in prison, mum.'

'Bravo, Hannah. Bravo.'

She looks at me as though I've morphed into the devil.

'What about those things they found on his computer?'

'It wasn't abuse. They always throw that card out. It was a relationship. A mutual affection. Silly girl probably thought it was love.'

'Who? Mum, you're not making any sense. Are you saying you know who he *did* abuse?'

I cram another handful of crisps into my mouth.

'You could have done something. But instead, you let my father rot in prison for three weeks, released after God knows what happened to him in there, get so depressed that he couldn't see another way out and hang himself with a set of jump leads. Is that what you're saying?'

She wouldn't understand. How could she?

'Nobody knows what I've been through. Nobody cares.'

'Are you drunk?'

'I don't drink, you know that. Not with the diabetes.'

She doesn't say what is visible behind her hard glare. I know what she's thinking. Why am I eating crap on top of insulin? The truth is, I don't give a fuck anymore. That's why.

'Then what are you talking about?'

'I know what rape feels like.'

She looks visibly shaken by my confession.

'My father. What he did to me is no better than what that teacher did to your father, God rest his soul.'

'You're saying you and dad . . . were abused?'

'I like to think that's what connected us.'

We were alright until Sophie made those false allegations.

'Everything would have continued as normal if she hadn't come along, trying to build your father a grave for his hard-earned money.'

Hannah doesn't disagree, allowing me to continue.

'And look where that got her? Dead and buried just like your soppy father. Taking his own life, what was he thinking? Stupid bugger.'

Hannah jolts at my words and rises up out of her chair.

'Oh, hear me out.'

'If you know something you ought to tell the police.'

'Sit down.'

'Why should I?'

'Don't you wanna know?'

She reluctantly returns to her seat. 'Why did you keep quiet if you knew my father was innocent?'

'I was raped. Buggered. Abused. By my own father. Your wonderful granddad. My mother did fuck all to stop it. She didn't even believe me.'

'That's why you left home and moved in with dad?'

I nod. '1987. He was twenty years old. He left that stupid band and started working at the aerospace.'

'What has this got to do with dad?'

'The phone. I should have thrown it away, but, it was my only lifeline. I don't get out much these days, you know that. Those messages to her. The internet searches.'

'You saw them?'

I shake my head at her ignorance.

'Antony could barely get a hard-on, let alone manage an affair-'

'An affair? It was rape.'

'So you keep saying.' I wave her concerns off with a brush of my hand through the air as I shift in my chair, but the weight of my skin is a lesser burden than the secret I've been carrying all these years.

'That thing with Kate, it wasn't how they made it look.'

'Kate? Who the fuck is Kate?'

I try to retract my words. 'I mean Sophie.'

'They made it look pretty terrible, mum.'

'They did, didn't they. We should sue them.'

'What?'

'It was harmless fun, nothing more. She wanted it.'

'Mum, you're making no sense. How could it be fun, she was a girl. A seven-year-old child. And how the hell could you know what happened to her? Were you there?'

She was fourteen, not seven.

I glance down to the floor. 'You're not listening.'

'You're talking in riddles.'

Leaning forward, placing her hand on my arm she says, 'look, what happened to you and dad, that's shit, but men like that don't deserve a wasted breath. They're screwed up. They destroy lives.'

'My father wasn't ill. He was a monster.'

'I'm saying he was sick. He must've been, right, to think it's okay to have sex with a child?'

'You're saying I'm not well. That I've got a screw loose.'

'Not you, Granddad, and that teacher who abused dad.'

'No, you're saying what Kate and I had was wrong. That her feelings for me were a figment of my imagination. That I abused her.'

Hannah looks as revolted as I feel at such an accusation.

'You and . . . Kate?'

Hannah flies out of the chair and heads towards the door. I don't have time to grab her. She's too quick. But she can't get far. The front door is locked. The key in my pocket. The knife up my sleeve.

As I ease out of the chair with my eyes fixed to the open door, Hannah panics and freezes. We both turn our heads to the window at the sound of a car approaching the road.

Even if they're coming for me the police won't be quick enough. By the time they force the door off its hinges I'll be dead. So will Hannah. Our throats slit just like Sophie's.

DI SILVER

I knock three times, but there's no answer.

'I'll take a look through the window,' says DI Locke.

I count to three before raising my hand to knock again, but Locke appears at my side, phone pressed to her ear.

'I need back-up, now. The Wells'.'

She turns to me and says, 'break the door down. She's got a knife.'

'Who?'

'Jacky's got a knife to her daughter's throat.'

I step back and begin to kick the door, but it doesn't budge. Noticing a plant pot on its side, still half-full of soil I crouch down, collect it from the ground, and in one swipe slam it down hard against the door. Soil and cracked pottery lie at my feet, but the door remains untouched.

Locke jumps in front of me, jimmies the lock with a key she finds beneath the mat on the path and in less than thirty seconds we're inside the house.

'Jacky?'

'Fuck off!' she says, swiping at me with the heel of a shoe.

I look down to see Hannah doubled over, clutching her chest.

'Did 'er a favour. And that stupid cunt Sophie.'

I don't have time to go over the reason why Jacky has chosen now to admit to killing Sophie. The blade handle is protruding from her daughter's chest.

'Drop the shoe Jacky,' says, Locke, the intensity of her gaze enough to make a grown man quiver in his boots.

'Do as she says, Jacky.'

'Fuck off!' she says, lunging at me with the heel aimed at my skull.

KATE

I can't move. I can't breathe. I'm frozen to the spot as I watch the two detectives marching Jacky Wells out of the house. To stand so close to the woman who ruined my childhood, damaged my sex life, tarred my relationship with my husband is too much.

A wave of nausea rises up from my stomach and into my throat. I lean forwards and throw up. Images of the sick things she did to me burn my eyes. Antony wasn't to blame. He didn't know. When he came into the bedroom to find me sat on the edge of the bed, shaking uncontrollably after Jacky had left me to clean myself up, he did what he thought was right. He covered me with a towel and held me to his chest as I wept. How was he supposed to know that she'd just molested me?

'What's wrong girl?' he said.

But I couldn't find the words to express what had happened, what she'd done.

I felt numb.

When I returned home that day, confused about my sexuality, unsure whether I'd asked for it, assuming I was somehow to blame, I did what any other fourteen-year-old girl would do. Unable to comprehend the way my body had reacted to her touch, I tried to pretend it didn't happen. I blocked it out, shoved it into a box, and hid it in the back of my head. Until the next time. And the time after that. Two years later, during a sex education lesson, I realised to my horror what I'd experienced wasn't normal.

That night I began to pull at my hair, ripping it out in clumps until I felt the satisfaction of pain. The bald spot grew back, but my self-harm became I way of making sense of my feelings. When I was numb I'd cut myself with razor blades. When I was angry I'd pull at my hair. Then later, as I grew older, I became obsessed with security, locking gates, doors, ensuring nobody could come in and get me.

Because of her.

Because of what she'd done to me.

She told me that she knew where I lived and that if I told anyone she'd set fire to the house and kill my family. I left home at the age of sixteen and never looked back.

She's the reason I haven't spoken to my parents in years.

She's the reason I lied to my husband.

She's being escorted into a police car because she's guilty.

She should feel ashamed, not I.

I close my eyes and when I open them, I see a half-formed moon. The stars twinkling in the night sky. The world around me remains just as it always has, but I know that from this moment on my life will never be the same.

TERESA

I drive along the ring road and straight across the roundabout to the house. I see blue lights flashing. Two police cars are parked over the drive preventing me from entering the quiet street. I emerge from the car to see a woman standing staring at the house where DI Silver and DI Locke are escorting Jacky into one of the vehicles. As I walk towards her I can see that her hands are covered in blood.

An ambulance turns the corner sharply, silent, lights flashing.

'Hannah?'

I run towards the house, but DI Locke prevents me from entering.

'You can't go in there. It's a crime scene.'

'Hannah?' I gulp back bitter realisation.

'She's going to be fine.'

'What happened? I want to see my granddaughter.'

'She's been stabbed. Her mother has been arrested. It looks like surface wounds. She's going to be okay.'

I crumple to the concrete, gathering my thoughts, my breath coming in ragged gasps as waves of relief wash over me.

I thought I was going to lose her.

I thought I was going to be alone.

It's this that forces me upright. The knowledge that I

am not alone. I never was. Hannah needs me. And so long as someone does, I will be okay.

The paramedics wheel the stretcher away from the house and down the path towards the open doors of the ambulance.

'I'm going with her.'

DI Locke nods to her colleague as I step into the vehicle, catching a glimpse of Hannah's wide-eyed stare.

'It's going to be okay,' I say, holding her cold, trembling hand. 'We can get through this together.'

She bites her lip as a single fat tear falls down her plump cheek.

I squeeze her hand tighter.

Before the doors close behind us I glance away from Hannah's pale, still body to see a woman walking into the shadows.

'Had a good enough look?'

She forces her head up straight, rolls back her shoulders, and walks with purpose down the narrow winding road.

Who is she and why was she staring at the house?

DI SILVER

Back inside the office, we're greeted by Dawson and Black, who offer us a congratulatory handshake. I don't feel like celebrating. Wells' life was cut short by a string of accusations that never lead to a trial; he took his own life before he could be punished for what he put those girls through. Sophie's body lies in a coffin awaiting burial. And Hannah is undergoing surgery to remove a knife from her torso that her own mother put there.

Locke removes her coat and heads towards the coffee machine. I stand beside her, lowering my voice as DI Blake and DI Flint walk past, a tray of homemade lemon sponge cake in hand.

'What do you make of Jacky's ramblings?'

'She's clearly suffering from some kind of mental breakdown.' She points to my face. 'Look what she did to your nose.'

I raise my hand to feel the bruise the heel of her shoe made as she flung it at me.

'You don't think there's anything more to it?'

Locke shakes her head. 'The paramedic said it might have something to do with her diabetes, her blood sugar levels going haywire or something.'

'She said Antony never did it, and that he never even spoke to Sophie.'

'Who knows what she meant by that.'

'I still think she knew what he was up to.'

She turns, places her hand on my arm and says, 'it's over.'

Forget about it; move on.

I nod. 'Okay.'

DCI Black moves towards me with a file of paperwork in his hand.

'I need you to prepare a statement for the nationals. They want to know how a media leak from one of our own might have contributed to the way they portrayed Antony's case.'

Great.

'Yes Guv.'

Locke lowers her gaze. 'I'll be at my desk if you need me.'

I hold out my hand to stop her as she turns.

'Take care not to divulge police business to reporters in future.'

I note the slight flush appear on her cheeks.

'We're dating.'

'Ah, I see.'

Deciding to change the subject she says, 'going for a drink later?'

'Will he be joining us?'

She smiles. 'Johnno's working tonight.'

'You buying?'

'Fine,' she says, raising her eyes to the ceiling.

I walk towards the desk, planting the reports down in front of me. I'm about to sit when the phone rings.

'No rest for the wicked, eh?' says Locke, her back turned to me as she crosses the room.

No, there isn't.

There will always be a victim coming forward, a perpetrator continuing with their life, oblivious that we're about to come knocking on their door. But so long as there are people like us, prepared to give the unheard a voice, the fight for justice will resume.

KATE

Four months later

The courtroom is silent. Steven sits to my right, Lisa to my left. Dylan beside his father. Everyone's eyes are on the bench, waiting for the verdict.

I took up DI Locke's suggestion for therapy. While my abuser orchestrated a story, I sat in a chair and divulged every sordid detail of my abuse in a safe, comfortable environment to a complete stranger.

The judge focuses her eyes on the accused and my heart begins to thud in my chest. I flick the elastic band on my wrist, hidden beneath a long sleeved jumper and feel the familiar sharp sting. A safe form of self-harm my therapist introduced me to.

When the judge begins to speak, Steven grips my hand a little tighter. Once the words have fallen from her lips there is no going back.

I glance around me at the others in the public gallery, where several reporters now stand, and catch Teresa looking at me. Her face etched with worry. So she should be. For birthing that dimwit who wasn't able to comprehend what his future wife was doing with a fourteen-year-old girl as he sat in the living room humming lyrics.

I catch two words from the judge.

Did I hear her right?

Steven turns and pulls me towards him. I lean into the soft fabric of his coat and exhale.

Guilty.

One count of murder against Sophie Anderson, and one count of attempted murder against her own daughter, Hannah.

At least she'll be off the streets.

Jacky ruined my childhood, but behind bars, for the next twenty years, she won't be given access to a computer. Unable to download images of children being abused for her own perverted pleasure she will have plenty of time to evaluate her past. Just as I have done.

TERESA

Twenty years.

It's no less than Jacky deserves.

I think of Antony, lying alone in the cold hard earth and I wonder what hell is like. They can both rot for all I care.

I reach out my hand towards Hannah, and we walk arm in arm out of the court.

I might not have been the best mother, but I can be a better grandmother to Hannah and her children.

Rachel Harper asked me if I'd ever be able to forgive my son. I told her that it was a work in progress. Much like accepting that I created a monster. You have to work at it. But I'm trying.

As we reach the steps a flash of royal blue catches my eye. I turn to meet the eyes of the woman I saw opposite the house the night Jacky, enraged, stabbed her daughter. I wonder if she too is a victim of my son's cruelty. Has she also survived the evil of abuse?

'Come on, nan. Let's grab a coffee. I'm parched.'

I smile and follow Hannah to the car.

ACKNOWLEDGEMENTS

I'd like to say a huge thank you, first of all, to my husband Michael, whose encouragement and advice made a huge difference to this title, especially the denouement.

Secondly, I must thank all the wonderful members of the Facebook Book Group: *Crime Fiction Addict* for the support they offer Indie author's, and a special mention to Fred and Betsy Reavley, David Gilchrist, Sue Leopold, Caroline Vincent, Maggie James, Judith Baker, Helen Claire, Sarah Kenny, Kerry Watts, Trish Dixon, Mark Tilbury, Susan Hunter, Barbarah Copperthwaite, Sandra Dean, Emma Mitchell, Jill Burkinshaw, Angela Rose, Caroline Maston, and of course, Valerie Holmes.

Thirdly, I must thank my beta readers and ARC reviewers for their objective honest literary criticism which continues to inspire and support my writing.

Lastly, I offer a huge thank you to my readers all over the world who have purchased my titles and for believing in me. Reviews are important to us, it helps other readers to find our work so please share your thoughts on Goodreads and Amazon, and recommend this title to a friend.